Book One of the Lady Blade Series:

The
Maestro's Daughter

by

Catherine Thrush

DEDICATION

To my first fencing maestro John DeCesare who loaned his name for characters in this book, my continuing fencing maestro Greg Chow and the whole fencing gang at Salle DeCesare.

May your aim be true, your point in line, and your timing perfect.

CONTENTS

ACKNOWLEDGEMENTS

Special thanks to all my friends in the Monday Night Writers and the Potluck Publishers who read these chapters as I wrote and rewrote them over and over and told me how bad they were—until they weren't. Thank you for your patience and your sage advice.

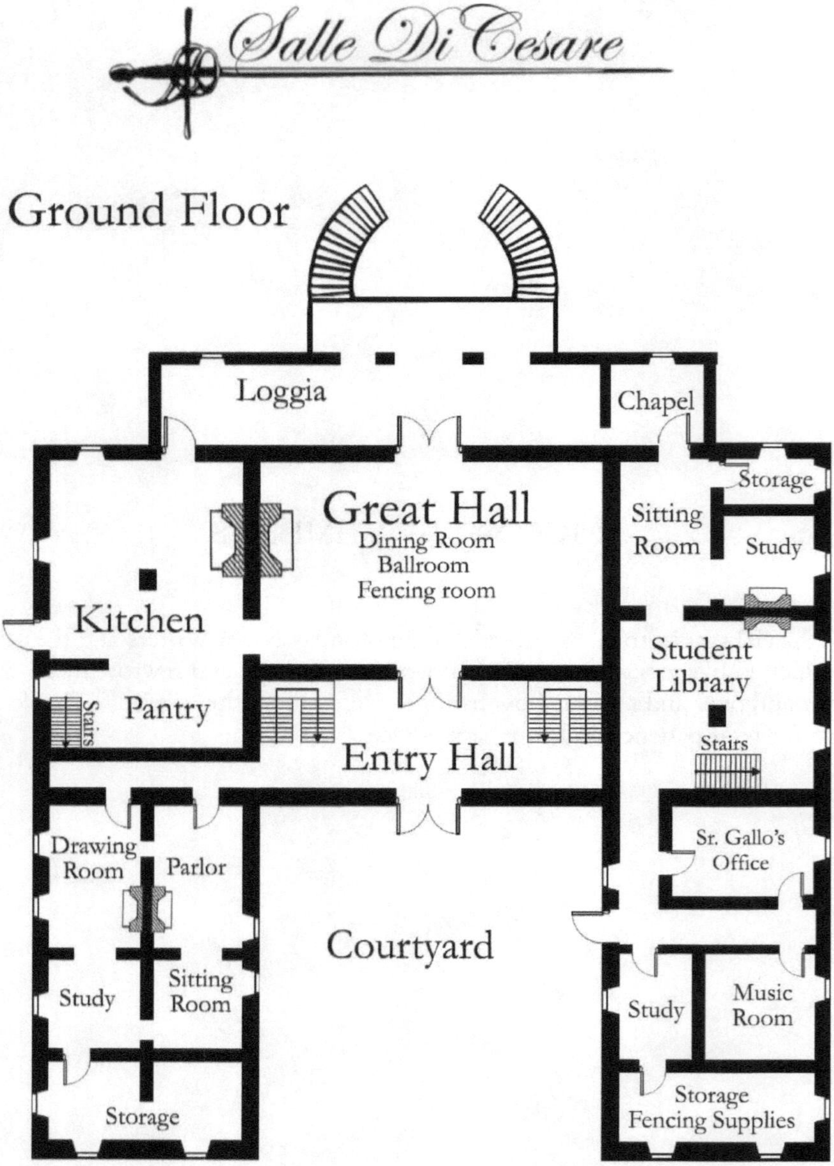

Ground Floor

Loggia

Chapel

Great Hall
Dining Room
Ballroom
Fencing room

Sitting
Room

Storage

Study

Kitchen

Student
Library

Pantry

Stairs

Entry Hall

Stairs

Drawing
Room

Parlor

Sr. Gallo's
Office

Courtyard

Study

Sitting
Room

Study

Music
Room

Storage

Storage
Fencing Supplies

First Floor

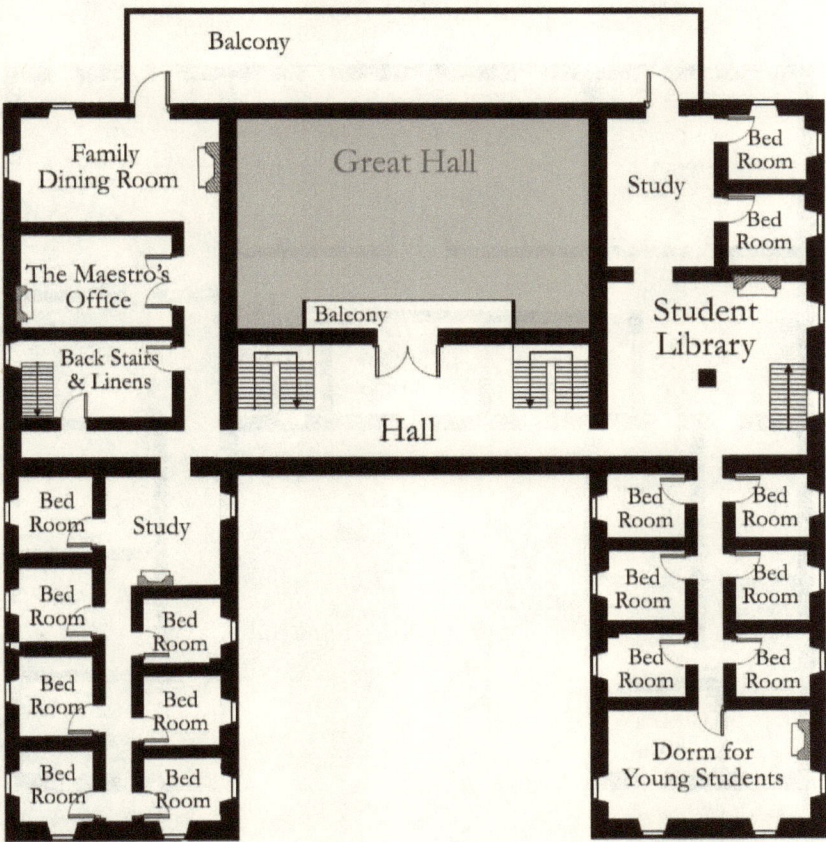

Balcony

Family Dining Room

Great Hall

Study

Bed Room

Bed Room

The Maestro's Office

Student Library

Back Stairs & Linens

Balcony

Hall

Bed Room

Study

Bed Room

Bed Room

Bed Room

Bed Room

Bed Room

Bed Room

Bed Room

Bed Room

Bed Room

Bed Room

Bed Room

Dorm for Young Students

Second Floor

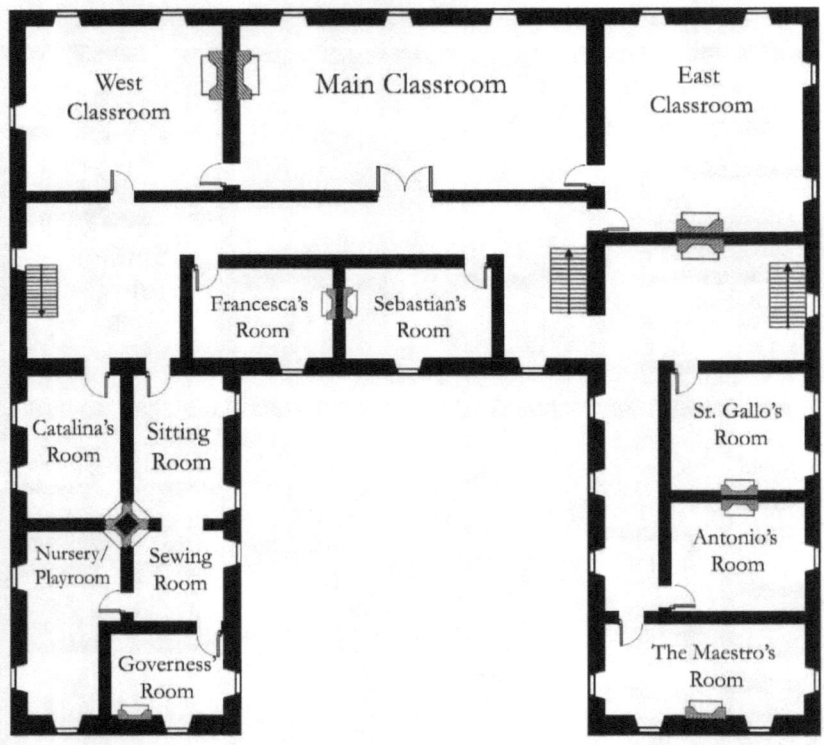

There is always one moment in childhood when the door opens and lets the future in.

Graham Greene

CHAPTER 1
THE GOLDEN BOY

Grand Duchy of Tuscany
May 10th, 1716

The clank and scrape of steel blades seemed sharper than usual to Francesca. Perhaps it was the chill in the bright spring air that carried the sound in through the window, or maybe it was because so much depended on the outcome of the fencing bout taking place in the cobblestone courtyard three stories below.

"I can't watch," said Catalina, Francesca's best friend. Catalina turned away from the window and sat on the edge of Francesca's bed. She smoothed and resmoothed her pale blue skirts and petticoats with long elegant fingers.

"Your brother will be fine. He's a good fencer," Francesca said, trying to sound more certain than she felt. *Enzo's quick with his blade,* she added to herself, *but impetuous, he's easily baited with a feint and hit on the counterattack.*

The knot of anxiety in Francesca's stomach grew as she turned back to the bout. Two dozen of Papa's fencing students filled the yard in a ring around Catalina's brother, Enzo and his opponent, Frederick. A few of the household staff who weren't busy looked on. The rowdy younger students clapped and shouted encouragement. The more serious older ones watched the action with calculating expressions, sizing up the fighters' skills. All the students wore padded canvas jackets over linen shirts and gripped metal fencing foils with blunted tips.

Papa moved along with the sparring pair. His frame, all lean, ropy muscle, kept equidistant from them, his movements light and agile and his eyes intent, judging the fairness of the bout. He wore a short, maestro's jacket and his brushed-back, black, shoulder-length hair, grayed at the temples.

Frederick dropped his sword arm, inviting Enzo to attack.

Don't do it, thought Francesca as she dug her fingernails into the windowsill. *Make him come to you.*

Enzo took the bait and lunged; sword extended. Frederick took a quick leap back so that Enzo's blade stopped an inch short of his chest. Before Enzo could recover, Frederick's blade flashed in the sun, gliding along the length of Enzo's blade pushing it out of line. The blunted tip landed on Enzo's side.

"Halt!" called Papa. "*Touché,* Frederick."

Francesca took a quick inhale, her stays suddenly feeling too tight. Catalina sprung from the bed and joined her at the window. Catalina's arched eyebrows drew together in a frown as she plucked at the ruffles at her sleeve. "What's happened?"

"Frederick landed another point. They're tied now, three to three."

"I can't stand this," Catalina said, wringing Francesca's arm.

"It's all right," Francesca said and put her hand over Catalina's. "The bout will go to at least five and the winner needs to win by two points. There's time yet."

If Enzo lost, he'd have to leave the school and Catalina would go with him.

Since Francesca was the only girl in a houseful of men, her grandmother had insisted years ago on a companion for her—a girl near Francesca's age and social status. Catalina had come to keep Francesca company and help as needed—in exchange for her brother's admission to the salle. Francesca couldn't bear to lose her, especially now when she still felt so raw from her grandmother's death six months ago.

But there was nothing either of them could do. Francesca's helplessness grated against her taut nerves.

"It seems so unfair to send someone away for losing a silly fencing match," Catalina said, as tears formed in the corners of her eyes.

There's nothing silly about fencing, thought Francesca, knowing Catalina would huff and toss her head if she said so. "It's not just one match, but I know Enzo will win," Francesca said instead. A pupil had to lose a series of matches in order to be sent home.

Francesca understood that Papa had to maintain the prestige of his fencing school by admitting only the best and brightest pupils. After all, he was Maestro DiCesare, premier master in the art and science of defense. Each student had to earn his place both in fencing and academics. But at the moment, it seemed like a hard policy to accept.

The villa, Salle DiCesare, formed a horseshoe around the noisy courtyard. To her right in the yard, a faded canvas awning covered wood benches, racks of fencing gear, and mannequins used for practice. Past the courtyard stood the main, wrought-iron gate in the stone wall that surrounded the grounds, and beyond stretched the stables, the dueling grounds, and the emerald, rolling hills of Tuscany. Francesca tried not to imagine a carriage carrying Catalina away into those hills.

She brought her attention back to the bout. Enzo and Frederick stood in *en garde* position, knees bent, back straight, right shoulders forward and sword arms ready. Frederick was from the north, light-skinned and brown-haired whereas Enzo was tanned, with dark hair. Enzo, the taller of the two, had greater reach. He was also quicker, but Frederick was smarter. And while Francesca was rooting for Enzo, one of the things she loved most about fencing was that brains often proved more effective than brawn.

This time, when Papa cried "Fence," Enzo and Frederick launched themselves at each other simultaneously. They came together with a clank of blades and grunts of surprise.

"Halt!" Papa turned to Francesca's eldest brother, Antonio, who stood among the watching students. "Did you see who began the action?"

Antonio often served as judge during bouts and teacher for the younger students. Wiry and athletic, Antonio took after Papa, not only in build, but also in his jet-black hair. Papa said that Antonio was nearly a maestro himself and would be one in a few years' time. He'd certainly mastered *acting* superior—at least to Francesca.

Antonio and Papa conferred for a moment. Papa put a hand on Antonio's shoulder as they spoke. It was such a little thing, really. Papa did it unconsciously and Antonio didn't even seem to notice, but a bitter taste lodged at the back of Francesca's throat. Antonio had no idea how lucky he was; how much she longed to be down there, attending class in the sunny courtyard with Papa and taking part in the competition.

Antonio towered over their brother, Sebastian, who stood nearby cheering Enzo on. Sebi was a year older than Francesca, and his head of unruly auburn curls was the same color as hers. He also had her green eyes and square jaw. At sixteen he already had a thicker chest and more solid build than Antonio.

Papa turned back to the opponents. "The point is Enzo's. The score stands at four to three. *En garde* gentlemen."

"You can do it, Enzo," whispered Catalina. "Just one more point." Her grip on Francesca's arm tightened.

Come on Enzo, thought Francesca. *Wait for him to attack, then do a double disengage. Frederick falls for that every time.*

Enzo seemed to have read her thoughts. When the action started, he backed off and waited for Frederick to make the first attack. Frederick obliged and lunged in. Nearly too quick to see, Enzo beat Frederick's blade to the side. As Frederick moved to parry Enzo's return strike, Enzo flicked his blade to the other side of Frederick's and landed his point squarely on Frederick's chest.

"Halt!" called Papa. "Gentlemen, the point and the match go to Enzo."

"Thank goodness!" Francesca said as she and Catalina hugged, the top of Catalina's head coming only up to her cheek. Below, the crowd of students moved in to congratulate Enzo and console Frederick.

"What a relief," Catalina said.

Francesca exhaled as the knots in her shoulders and jaw loosened. *At least until next year,* she thought to herself.

"I'd better get back downstairs before Signora Bianchi realizes I'm gone," Catalina said. Francesca nodded. No one was better at slipping past their governess than Catalina, but even she couldn't push her luck too far. Catalina was supposed to be helping the chambermaids melt wax for candle making and Francesca was supposed to be in the kitchen garden planting herbs.

Catalina hurried to the door, "I'll see you at our Latin lesson, mistress."

"Don't—" the door clicked closed behind Catalina, "Call me that." Francesca hated that title, especially from Catalina. It brought to mind Nana's death—which had made Francesca "mistress" of the salle—of how much she missed Nana and the myriad responsibilities she'd inherited.

Still, she found ways to make time for the important things. The herbs could wait a little. She turned back to the window, braiding her long hair.

Below, celebration and commiseration were over. Now the students filled one side of the courtyard. They stood in line, rigidly at attention, backs straight, right shoulders forward, their sword tips touched the ground in front of them as they waited for class to begin.

Francesca hurried to her bed, knelt, pushed aside the peach brocade bedspread, and pulled a rusted and bent practice blade from beneath it. She positioned herself near the window, just out of sight of those below. She tucked up her cream-colored skirts and dropped into *en garde* position.

She obeyed Papa's commands as they floated up from the courtyard. "Advance. Retreat. Parry. Lunge." She worked across the terracotta tiles of her bedroom floor from her carved oak armoire to her bed and bookcase and back again, ten steps each way.

Happiness hummed in the back of her mind as she concentrated on her footwork, stretched into each lunge, and checked her form. Her mind sharpened. Only fencing made her feel so grounded, focused, and so exhilarated.

Papa called a halt and Francesca returned to the window with her blade hidden behind her.

Papa had the students pair off to practice their attacks and low parries, *seconda* and *mezzo cerchio*. He called on her brothers to demonstrate.

Francesca drew a torn canvas jacket stuffed with pillows and stockings from under her bed. She propped up the dummy on her bed, took her *en garde* position, and practiced lunging, spearing her point into it.

After low parries they worked on timed attacks and disengages. It was frustrating not to have a blade to parry against, but Francesca practiced as best she could in the cramped space of her bedroom against her plump opponent—who chose the worst times to topple over.

Amid the sound of blades, Papa's voice moved among the students and wafted up to her. "Men, you must learn more than footwork and bladework. A man is not defined by his arm, nor by how many enemies he vanquishes. What is it that earns respect and authority? What sets man apart from the beasts? What makes us fit to sit at the knees of God in the hereafter?"

"Honor!" Francesca and the students said in unison.

"You are all young men of privilege or means," Papa went on, "but privilege bestowed can be taken away. Wealth can be lost as well as won. The only treasure that is yours and yours alone is your honor. Guard it well and you will always be rich men."

As Francesca righted her dummy yet again, Papa called, "Halt! Take a rest, men."

A buzz of voices rippled across the courtyard, and she hurried to the window.

Two riders on horseback approached along the dirt road that twisted up the hill between the silver-green olive grove and the winter brown of the vineyards.

From her third-story vantage, Francesca thought at first that the lead rider wore a gold helmet, but it was a head of golden hair. Most likely he was another nobleman's son, a pupil for Papa. She guessed him to be near Sebastian's age, a year or two older than her. The second rider wore servant's garb.

Francesca's interest grew as the golden-haired boy cantered up on his white horse. A hint of silver glittered from the rider's waistcoat beneath a sea-blue coat. He wore a sword at his side and black boots. His skin was smooth and pale except for his ruddy cheeks. There was a lithe elegance to the way he rode and the way he casually saluted the company as he approached. He was the most beautiful young man she had ever seen.

Papa opened the gate, and the young man rode into the courtyard. He hailed Papa in English, then swung gracefully out of the saddle. With a bow he presented a folded paper to Papa.

As Papa read, the boy's gaze swept over the other pupils then across the walls of the salle. Francesca ducked back behind her sheer drapes as her heart beat faster. She shook her head at her foolishness. What did another pupil more or less mean to her anyway—except another student who might send Enzo and Catalina packing? But she watched from behind the sheer curtain anyway.

Papa folded the paper. "Lord Worthington, I've been expecting you," he said in English. "I see that you studied in London under Sir William Hope."

At the name of William Hope Francesca leaned forward intently and the students exchanged looks. Most of them didn't speak English, but a translation of Maestro Hope's book, *The Scots Fencing Master*, was required reading at the salle. A dog-eared copy also lay hidden under Francesca's bed.

"Yes, sir, I studied with him for a year," the young man said.

"A fine gentleman and a friend," Papa said, smiling. "It will be advantageous to familiarize the other pupils with the Scottish style of fence. Why did you leave his school?"

"Through no wish of mine, sir. Unexpected family business took me away."

"I see," Papa said. "And what weapons have you studied?"

"Back sword as well as rapier and dagger, sir."

"Well, it's a start. You must be tired after your journey." Papa motioned to Antonio. "My son Antonio will see you are made comfortable."

"Thank you, signore," Lord Worthington said.

"You may call me Maestro. All students here are treated equally regardless of title."

"Of course, Maestro." The youth made a curt nod.

As Antonio ushered the new student through a doorway into the far wing of the villa, Francesca heard a familiar *clip clack clip* in the hallway. Panic swept through her. She recognized the footsteps of her governess, Signora Bianchi.

Francesca shoved the foil and fencing dummy deep under her bed. She grabbed a book at random from her bookshelf and laid it open on the bedspread. She was just yanking her skirts into place when a sharp knock came at her door. She took a breath, let it out slowly, then opened the door.

"Good day, signora," Francesca said softly with her prettiest smile.

Signora Bianchi looked down her long nose at Francesca. She was a painfully thin woman. Her slender face and her bony arms with knobby joints reminded Francesca of a stork, and her choice of white and black clothing did nothing to dispel the impression.

"Francesca, I've just come from the garden, the un-planted garden. Really, child. It's a simple task. What have you been up to?"

Francesca feigned surprise. "Goodness, signora, I'm so sorry! I was reading the book Papa gave me and lost track of the time." She glanced over to see what book she had grabbed in case she was questioned. *A New Voyage Round the World* by William Dampier. Luckily, she practically knew the text by heart.

"That," Signora Bianchi said with a superior air, "is why I discourage reading in young women. It distracts them from their duties and puts outlandish ideas in their heads."

Francesca bit back a tart reply. To the signora, any thought not about household duties was "outlandish."

The signora shook her head. "No time for the herbs now. You have kept the schoolmaster waiting. It is past time for your Latin lesson."

She turned on her heels and headed back down the hall toward the schoolroom.

"I am so sorry, signora," Francesca said and fell in step beside her.

"I should think so. But I am not the only one you must apologize to."

Francesca nodded dutifully. "I shall offer Signor Gallo my sincerest regrets."

They stopped outside the schoolroom.

"See that you do. Afterwards you will work in the garden, and then join Signora Morella and me in the pantry. Now that you've learned the management of the dairy, it's time you learned the management of the kitchen and larder. We'll inventory the pantry and discuss ordering procedures. Then you'll assist Chef Amico for the next two weeks."

Francesca felt as though she'd swallowed a lead ball. *Two more weeks of drudgery!* She put on a smile. "Thank you, signora. I look forward to it."

As she opened the schoolroom door her mind skipped back to the boy who had joined the salle, young Lord Worthington. He reminded her of an angel from an illustration she'd seen in one of Papa's books, golden and shining. *He's probably like all the others: dull, snobbish, and superior.* But she hoped not.

CHAPTER 2
NIGHTMARES

That night Francesca crept from her room and closed the oak door softly behind her. Her heart pounded as she stood, back to the door, hoping her eyes would readjust. Compared to her moonlit chamber, the hall was a black void. A draft brushed her sweat-soaked skin, raising goosebumps on her arms.

She'd had the nightmare again. As always, she'd been trapped in a windowless, doorless stone chamber. Black water poured from the walls and rapidly filled the room. She pounded uselessly on the walls. Then her feet left the floor, and she was treading water. She screamed for help. Soon her head bumped against the ceiling, but the water still rose. Scaly, half-seen creatures, part fish, part toothy imp, filled the dark water. They bit and clawed at her. Then she was underwater, fighting for air as the creatures pulled her down, down, down. There was no bottom.

She had woken panicked, tangled in her sheet, struggling to get free. She'd pulled on her clothes, thrown a shawl over her shoulders, and hurried out of the room.

"It was just a dream," she whispered aloud to the empty hallway, but she felt their claws on her legs and suppressed a shudder.

She took a deep breath and squared her shoulders. "A *stupid* dream," she said a little louder in defiance of the creatures.

She'd had the same dream about once a week, ever since Nana died, so she knew she couldn't go back to bed. The nightmare would be there waiting. She'd found only one cure—her horse, Achilles.

Going to the stable in the middle of the night was risky. If the night watchman caught her, she'd likely spend weeks confined to her room as punishment, but she could handle that. It certainly wouldn't be the first time. And better a danger she could see and circumvent than a horror she couldn't control.

The villa was quiet except for the occasional creak of timbers and the sigh of the breeze. She had no idea what time it was, sometime after midnight she guessed.

She moved silently down the hall, trailing the fingers of her right hand along the smooth wood and marble wainscoting on the wall, and expertly avoiding the creaky floorboards. With her eyes nearly useless in the dark, her sense of smell sharpened. She picked out the harsh scent of the lye soap used to scour the floorboards and the smooth smell of linseed oil freshly rubbed on wood trim.

She passed a door on the opposite wall that she sensed as a yawning gap—the empty main school room. A few steps later her fingers brushed the door frame to Sebastian's room, and ten paces beyond Sebi's doorway were the stairs.

She reached the ground floor two flights down. A trail of filtered moonlight from the doorway to the great hall led her on. She shivered as she tiptoed through the gloomy vastness of the hall, into the closeness of the kitchen still smelling of onions and braised lamb, and out the oak door.

The kitchen gardens glowed blue in the moonlight, bright after the darkness inside. A band around her chest seemed to loosen. She took a deep breath, let it out slowly, and savored the scent of the sage and rosemary that she'd planted that afternoon. Despite the risk, or maybe because of it, she loved being out at night.

Rows of tilled dirt showed where she'd worked in the garden and tinted the air with the smell of freshly turned earth. Beyond the garden, moonlight glinted off the tile roof of the grounds-servants' quarters and the thatched roofs of the chicken coops and kennels.

Watching her steps, she headed silently toward the main gate. She paused as she rounded a corner of the villa and saw the watchman's golden lantern disappear around the far wing. She tiptoed through the open iron gate and hurried to the stable.

The interior of the stable was pitch black, but the familiar smell of horses and hay reassured her. She trailed her fingers along the rough wood to Achilles' stall two doors down. As she entered, he nickered in greeting. When she put her arms around his neck, the grip of the nightmare slackened. She breathed in his warm scent and her shoulders relaxed. Achilles rumbled deep in his wide chest and nuzzled her.

"Why do I always feel better with you? Huh, boy?" She stroked his arched Arabian neck and sighed. "Maybe because I know we can run away from anything. Nothing can hurt me when I'm on your back. I'm free."

Free. She recalled the last time she had felt that way—a sunny morning, eight months ago. She had run down the stairs to her grandmother's room.

Light slanted in from the half-drawn drapes and pooled on the oriental rug. Nana, recovering from winter fever, looked like a tiny, fragile doll in her big feather bed, but her eyes lit up and she patted the comforter with a wrinkled hand when Francesca appeared.

Francesca had just been released from a week confined to her room. The punishment had been completely unfair. Her governess had found her reading a book about the pygmy tribes of Africa, demanded she hand it over, and called it sacrilegious. Francesca had argued, strenuously. She felt the book was educational, and Sebi and Antonio had already read it, so why couldn't she?

She had appealed to Papa, who had come down on Francesca's side on the book, but on the signora's side on Francesca's "sassing" and "willfulness."

Finally released, Francesca had thrown herself onto Nana's bed.

"Mind you don't bounce me out, child," Nana said with mock sternness.

"Sorry. I'm just so happy to be free! I could have chewed through my bedroom door."

Nana laughed as she brushed hair from Francesca's eyes. "I don't doubt it. Even as a babe in your mother's belly you were always trying to kick your way out."

"Was I? Really?" Papa was always reluctant to speak of her mother, who had died when Francesca was born, so she treasured every tidbit.

"Why do you think we named you Francesca?" Nana said, "It means 'free one.'"

"That I am, at least for the moment." She rolled onto her back and spread her arms wide.

Nana took her hand. "I know you chafe at Signora Bianchi's strict rule, but she wants what's best for you."

"She won't let me *do* anything."

"None of us are free to do as we please. And believe me, child, she's less harsh than public opinion, and more apt to forgive."

"But it's not fair." Francesca grumbled.

Nana squeezed her hand. "Life is very seldom fair. Difficult as it might be, you need to learn to bend your nature to fit your station, because the world is not going to change to fit you."

Nana had passed a month later.

Francesca scratched Achilles' ears absently in the dark. That seemed like such a long time ago now.

"Well, I may not have learned to bend my nature, but I've gotten better at hiding it. Except with you. I never have to pretend with you."

She leaned her forehead against him for a moment. "You don't mind if I stay here, do you?" she scratched his ear. "Just a little while. I won't take up much room."

His soft muzzle grazed her cheek and she smiled.

Once Francesca's eyes adjusted to the dark, she piled hay in the corner of the stall to sleep on, but before she could lie down, the stable door slid open, admitting a wash of moonlight. She crouched and held her breath.

The door closed again, and the darkness deepened. She heard a rustle of clothing and a masculine chuckle that sounded like Sebastian. What was he up to? He wasn't supposed to be out of bed any more than she was.

A pair of muted voices moved toward her down the aisle. As they passed Achilles' stall, she heard a feminine giggle that she knew well—Catalina.

Her mouth dropped open in shock. Catalina wasn't above sneaking past Signora Bianchi on occasion, but this!

Sebi laughed as well. "Leave some for me."

Jealousy and hurt lodged in her chest. Usually, Catalina chided her for bending the rules, but here she was, breaking them to pieces with Sebi. Francesca had thought Catalina was worried about Enzo's match because she didn't want to lose their friendship, but maybe it was Sebi she didn't want to lose. Maybe Catalina didn't care about her at all.

Francesca stood, voice trembling with hurt and betrayal. "Are you—"

Startled, Catalina gave a yelp and Sebi cursed.

"Hush! It's me, Francesca," she whispered, glancing nervously at the barn door.

"Mistress!" said Catalina, breathless.

"Please don't call me that," Francesca said, irritation joining the emotions stinging her eyes. She could barely make out Catalina's form in the dim light.

"What are you doing here?" demanded Sebi.

"I..."

"It was the dream again, wasn't it?" Concern softened Catalina's voice.

Francesca couldn't make out Catalina's eyes in the low light, but she could imagine her sympathetic look. She'd seen it often enough, and she felt slightly better.

But Sebi was there too, and Francesca didn't want to give him anything to tease her about. He could be relentless. "I just wanted to check on Achilles."

"What are you two up to?" she said, accusation sharpening her voice.

Liquid sloshed. "Catalina nipped a bottle of Madera that Papa tossed out," Sebastian said.

"And you had to drink it in the stable in the middle of the night? Or were you planning on feeding it to your horse?" snapped Francesca.

An awkward silence followed. Francesca sensed Catalina move closer to Sebi.

It wasn't fair. Sebi could do as he pleased and go where he chose. He had a dozen friends both at the salle and in town. Francesca wasn't allowed to do anything, and Catalina was her only friend, other than Achilles. She wouldn't share her with Sebi. He could find someone else to drink wine with in the dark.

"It's difficult to find someplace where we can be alone during the day," Sebi said.

"That's because you're not supposed to," Francesca snapped.

"Oh, and you're supposed to be in the stable in the middle of the night," he shot back.

"You're going to get Catalina sent away. Remember what happened to Viola?"

Francesca had heard rumors that Papa had ordered the chamber maid to leave the salle in disgrace, though she'd been eleven at the time and no one had explained why. She'd made the mistake of asking her governess, who scowled and told her that wickedness had no place in a proper household and never to mention Viola's name again.

"Goodness!" Catalina said, "We're not…"

"That was Antonio's fault," Sebi replied. "Besides, it's none of your business."

"It is my business. She's *my* friend. I don't want her to be sent away," Francesca said, her voice rising. "I can't—"

"Hush, please! Both of you!" hissed Catalina. "Why must you always fight? No one is going anywhere as long as you keep your voices down."

A seam of light appeared around the stable door. Francesca thrust open the door to Achilles' stall and Catalina and Sebastian piled in. They crouched with their backs against the stall door as someone, most likely the night watchman, wandered in, lantern in hand. The light gleamed yellow off Achilles' onyx coat and glittered in his dark eyes. The other horses snorted and stamped. The man whistled softly as he wandered up the aisle to the tack room then back toward the door.

Francesca glanced at Catalina and was annoyed to see she was holding Sebi's hand.

The man's exit plunged the stable back into the dark. All three of them let out their breath. Francesca sat down in the hay and felt Catalina and Sebi do the same.

"That was close," Sebi said.

The liquid sloshed again, and Francesca guessed Sebi was taking a drink. Something cool touched her arm. She grabbed the bottle and took a sip. She stifled a cough at the sour taste. No wonder Papa had thrown it away. She handed it back as her eyes readjusted. "How can you drink that?"

"It's not so bad," Sebi said.

"Francesca's right," Catalina said, "none of us should be out here. It was a bad idea. We should go back in."

"I, I think I'll stay here," Francesca said as Achilles nuzzled her. She scratched him behind the ear.

"Are they as bad as that?" Catalina asked.

"What 'they?'" asked Sebi.

"Francesca's nightmares."

Francesca shot her a dirty look that she probably couldn't see in the dark. Her secret was out now. "Nightmare," Francesca said. "Just one, always the same." She shivered.

"Well, what's it about?" asked Sebi.

"I don't want to talk about it." The dream was still too fresh in her mind and talking about it would make it more real.

"It must be bad if you're willing to risk Papa's wrath coming out here."

Francesca shrugged.

"But then, you risk worse every day," Sebi went on. "Sometimes I think you're trying to get sent to Billy England, or worse, a convent. You know that's what would happen if they found out about your fencing, don't you?"

Francesca tensed and looked toward the dark shape of Catalina. Pain welled. Catalina must have betrayed her; she was the only one who knew.

Francesca caught a shake of Catalina's head that she couldn't interpret. Was Catalina telling her she hadn't said anything, or not to admit anything?

She tried to sound unconcerned. "I don't know what you mean."

"Don't play innocent. I know you play at fencing in your room while we practice outside," Sebi said. "You've been doing it for what, three years?"

A band of iron tightened around Francesca's chest. Sebi was sure to tell Papa. "You're mistaken, I, I—"

"Rest easy," Sebi said. "I won't tell. It's nothing to me if you want to waste your time."

Catalina touched her arm again. "Upon my soul, I never said a word."

"She didn't need to," Sebi said. "Every time there's a demonstration you appear at your window. As soon as we start the exercise you disappear. What else would it be?"

The heat left Francesca's body. "Papa? Has he—"

"He's too busy with the students to notice."

The band around her chest loosened, but she was angry with herself. She should have been more careful. If Sebi noticed, others could too. She would need to hide behind her curtain while watching. It would be more difficult to see the nuances, but better that, than getting caught.

She didn't mention that she had been practicing nine years, not three, ever since her seventh birthday. Not every day, of course, Signora Bianchi often had other chores or tasks Francesca couldn't worm her way out of, especially since Nana had passed. But any day she could.

Sebi leaned toward her. "Why do you do it? What's the point? Girls can't fence."

Francesca fought back sudden anger. "So everyone says, but it's not true. A girl can fence. I can. I'm just not allowed to."

He shrugged. "There's more to fencing than waving a blade around and doing footwork."

"Such as?"

"Like having the courage to stare death in the face."

Francesca's laugh was sarcastic, and she thought she saw Catalina roll her eyes.

"Then you can't fence either," she said, crossing her arms and glaring at Sebi's vague shape. "You've never used anything but practice blades."

"Not true. I've fenced Antonio and Papa, as well as a few others with sharps."

She threw a handful of hay at him. "Since all of you are still alive, I guess no one stared death in the face."

"You know what I mean. Fencing takes courage and honor and you're afraid of a silly dream."

"That's hardly fair," Catalina said.

"I'm plenty brave enough to fence."

Sebi smirked.

Fire flooded her face, and she balled her fists. "I'll prove it to you. I dare you to fence with me."

He chuckled. "Why would I do that?"

"To prove me wrong," she said. "If you know so much, let's see it."

Her fingers itched to land a blade tip on his chest and wipe off the smugness she knew was on his face. She couldn't wait to show him what she had learned.

But out of nowhere, the horrible thought that he might be right blossomed in her mind and her stomach gave a lurch. She'd been told all her life that girls couldn't fence, but she'd always dismissed it as male rubbish meant to discourage her. But what if it wasn't?

"That seems like another bad idea," Catalina said.

"And if I'm right?" Sebi said. "If you can't fence, what then?"

A chill swept through Francesca, but she set her jaw. "If you're right, I'll give up. I will never touch a blade again." She tilted her head to one side. "Unless you're afraid you might be beaten by a girl."

Sebi snorted. "I suppose I'd be doing you a favor by showing you the truth."

Electricity jumped through Francesca. "You'll do it?" She started to rise, "I'll get the foils."

Something caught at her skirt. "No," Sebi said. "I'll get them. I'll be in a lot less trouble if I'm caught. Stay here."

"May I just say again that I think this is a terrible idea?" Catalina said.

"You may," Sebi said as the stall door opened and shut behind him.

"Please don't do this, mistress," Catalina said.

"You used to call me Franny," Francesca said. "I know you have to call me mistress in front of the signoras, but why do you have to when we're alone?"

"Because that's who you are now."

"I don't want to be! I want to be Franny. I want things to go back to the way they were. I wish..." She hunched her shoulders. She wished Nana hadn't died, leaving her a hundred new responsibilities, but it seemed childish to say so.

"I wish she were still here too," Catalina said softly.

Francesca rubbed her chest at the ache of Nana's absence.

"But what happens if you win this dare?" Catalina said. "How will anything be different?"

"What do you mean?"

"Even if you *can* fence, that doesn't mean you'll be allowed to. Nothing will change except you'll be even more unsatisfied."

"But I'll know!" Francesca was surprised by the emotion that flooded her. "I'll—"

The stable door opened again, washing Achilles in a trickle of golden light. Sebi opened the stall door with a hooded lantern and two foils tucked under his arm.

"I saw Signor Acardi heading back toward the gardens, so he'll be gone for a while," he said. "If we're going to do this, now is the time."

A thrill swept through Francesca as she leapt to her feet.

Sebi handed the lantern to Catalina and one of the practice blades to Francesca. "Remember," he said, "I'm doing this for your own good."

Francesca nodded as her body shook in anticipation. She faced Sebi in the aisle next to Achilles' stall. As she took her *en garde* position, her heart tried to beat its way out of her chest. She'd never faced anyone before but her stuffed mannequin. Her senses heightened and thrummed as Sebi lifted his blade and pointed it at her throat.

"Fence!"

CHAPTER 3
LOST IN TRANSLATION

Lightning ripped through Francesca. Elation flared. Lantern light gleamed off the blades. Everything seemed unnaturally clear and sharp.

As the tip of Sebi's blade moved toward her, seemingly in slow motion, every fencing move she had ever learned leapt into her mind at once. The advance, the retreat, the lunge, the crossover, the *patenando*, the *bulestra*, the *passato sotto* and a dozen others all fought to be first. Her body tried to go forward, backward, and sideways all at once, and lurched awkwardly onto the point of Sebi's weapon. His blunted blade jabbed sharply into her ribs.

She tried to do a retreat and a crossover retreat at the same time. Her feet got caught up, and she pitched backwards. Her ankle twisted beneath her, and she fell.

Francesca sat on the brick, hay-strewn floor. How could it have gone so horribly wrong?

"Well, that answers that question," Sebi said as he took the blade from her unresisting hand.

"But…" Francesca said. Were they right? Was it possible that despite years of practice she couldn't fence, would never be able to? Was there some *thing*, some defect in her body or mind that prohibited her from fencing simply because she was born a girl? Papa had once told her as much, but she hadn't believed him.

Tears gathered in her eyes, and she blinked them away quickly. After such a horrendous failure, she couldn't let Sebi see her cry. That would make her humiliation worse.

Sebi approached Catalina, extinguished the lantern, and plunged them all into darkness. "It's high time we all went back to bed."

Catalina helped her to her feet, and Francesca hissed as pain shot up her calf. Catalina put an arm around her.

"I'm sorry, Franny," Catalina said as she helped her toward the stable door. "At least now you know."

She was thankful for the darkness, so Sebi couldn't see her cry.

When Francesca woke the next morning, she pulled the covers over her head and contemplated never getting out of bed again. How could she ever face Sebi after last night? And what was there to get out of bed for? Kitchen work? Sewing? Pantry inventory?

She couldn't fence. That had become abundantly clear. She felt as if some vital part of her had been ripped away leaving a ragged hole. Without fencing, her life would become one dreary task after another if Signora Bianchi had anything to say about it.

She ignored Catalina's gentle knock on her door, hoping she'd go away, but she entered anyway.

"Leave me be," Francesca said from under the covers.

Catalina pulled back the sheet with a scowl between her perfectly arched eyebrows. "Don't you think you're being overly dramatic?"

"No," Francesca said, but she sat up and swung her legs out of bed. Signora Bianchi would make her get up soon anyway. If she had to dress and face the world, she'd rather have Catalina's cheerful help than the signora's unsympathetic glare.

Francesca stood, sucked in a breath as pain blossomed in her ankle and foot, and sat back down. Her ankle had bruised overnight. She growled at her traitorous limb for adding injury to insult. She'd hear no end of this from Sebi.

Catalina twisted her mouth to one side. "I guess you'll have to fall down the stairs again."

Francesca nodded. "I'm running out of books to sacrifice."

"Well, then you'll have to stop giving yourself injuries that we can't explain," Catalina said as she helped Francesca dress. "Honestly, I don't understand what the fuss is about fencing anyway."

Francesca held her tongue as the ragged hole yawned a little wider. She could see how foolish it must look. To Catalina fencing was nothing more than a way for boys to show off. But Francesca saw the noble art and the science; the perfect combination of mind and body, thought and action. And she saw her family's heart and soul. How could she explain that? She wasn't sure she understood herself, but the need to fence was as real as the stays and laces drawing tight around her torso, and just as binding.

Seated before her dressing-table mirror as she combed her auburn hair, Francesca stared at the girl looking back at her. At least the gaping hole didn't show. She looked the same as yesterday.

She wasn't pretty like Catalina. Her jaw was a little too square, her dark eyebrows a bit too straight and thick, her shoulders a little too broad for a girl. That was fine with her. Most of the boys left her alone, except for Burckhardt. Better that, than having the boys chase after her as they did Catalina.

Francesca envied Catalina's contentment. Not that her friend had it easy; the signoras were equally hard on her, but Catalina never seemed to long for more than life had allotted her. Francesca always wanted what was next, what was more, whatever lay around the corner or over the horizon—all the things promised her brothers and denied her. She rubbed her hands down her face. *Why did I have to be a girl?*

"I'll straighten up and be down in a minute," Catalina said as Francesca hobbled toward the staircase gritting her teeth at the pain. She carried three of her least favorite schoolbooks. She limped half-way down the stairs, then raised the books high and dropped them. They made a convincing racket as they thumped down the stairs and splayed open on the dark wood floor. Francesca limped quickly down to the bottom step, sat, and wrapped her hands around her sore ankle.

Papa was the first to appear around the corner from the dining room, followed by Antonio. Sebi brought up the rear.

Papa hurried to her. Concern puckered his graying brows and the scar that ran down his broad forehead, skipped his left eye, and continued down his cheek. Another scar slanted across his prominent right cheekbone— remnants from his days as a soldier and a duelist. He pursed his lips. "Cesca, my dear, are you hurt?" He pushed a few stray hairs back behind her ear.

"I'm fine, Papa," she replied as guilt pressed down on her.

"You are the clumsiest girl I've ever known." Antonio shook his head.

Sebi snickered in the background. Francesca wished she could dig her fingernails into his face.

"Perhaps you ought to wear padding." Antonio crossed his arms and leaned against the dark oak newel. "It seems like you tumble down the stairs every other week."

Papa shot Antonio a look as he took her hands and helped her up. She groaned when she put weight on her ankle. That part required no acting.

Papa had her sit down. He removed her shoe and examined her ankle, gently moving her foot around. Her cream wool stockings hid the bruises. "Tut, tut, tut," he said, shaking his head. "Sprained, I should think. I'll wrap it up and it'll be fine in a few days. Best keep your weight off of it for now."

"What happened last time?" Antonio said. "A dislocated finger?"

Francesca chewed at her lip. The finger was from a fall jumping Achilles over a hedge. Jumping had been forbidden after her previous spill, so she had ridden home, climbed the stairs cradling her hand, and pretended to trip down the steps. It was that or lose her riding privileges.

"That was the time before," Sebi said. "Last time was the gash in her arm."

Francesca's hand went to where the stitches had been, just below her elbow. That one was from a tumble from her favorite climbing tree.

"That's enough," Papa said. He gave Francesca a wink then turned to Sebi. "Bring Francesca some crutches."

"Yes, sir," Sebi said, hurrying off with a smirk.

Francesca put her arm around Papa's neck as he scooped her up and carried her toward their private dining room.

The students ate in the great hall downstairs under the watchful eye of the schoolmaster, but Papa insisted that the family dine together in a small room with wood-paneled walls, tapestries of domestic scenes in greens and golds, and a red marble fireplace. A painting of Francesca's red-haired mother hung above the mantle. Even when Nana had been bed-bound, Papa had instructed servants to carry her up in her wheeled chair for meals.

"Cesca, I've talked to you before about … reading on the staircases," Papa said.

Why the hesitation? Does he know I didn't fall? What does he think really happened?

"I'm sorry," Francesca said as she hugged him. That part was true. She was sorry for deceiving him, and somehow, though she was forbidden to fence, her failure made her feel like she had let him down. After all, she was a DiCesare. Fencing was in her blood—or ought to be.

Unfortunately, her injury was not deemed life-threatening enough to get her out of kitchen duty. She spent most of the day sweating on a chair next to the cookfire among the copper pots and pans. She turned a lamb on the rotisserie, stirred the soup kettle, and peeled vegetables, her leg propped on another chair. Even up and draped in a cool cloth, her ankle throbbed. Despite her busy hands, her mind kept going over and over her failure last night. *If only I'd had a little more time to prepare. I wasn't ready.* But she knew she was just making excuses. As Papa said, in a duel there are no second chances.

Lucia and Martina, the cook's maids, apologized for bumping into her as they tried to reach a particular pot or pan or dried herb that hung above her head. Francesca knew she was an irritation to them, but there was nothing she could do about it without angering Signora Bianchi.

Chef Amico, an energetic little man with a bristle-brush graying mustache and nimble hands that were constantly flourishing in the air, explained his every action to her as he boned a fish or tied up a roast. She tried her best to pay attention, but her mind invariably went back to that moment in the stable, looking up at Sebi's smug expression.

It didn't help when Sebastian popped in to gloat. "I see you found something you can actually *do*," he said with a wicked grin.

Francesca grasped the dead chicken she was plucking and strained not to throw it at him. She'd get endless lectures if she did. Still, it would almost be worth the bother. "What are you doing here?"

"Getting some carrots for Arrow. A few of us lads are riding into town."

Her grip on the half-plucked chicken tightened. She was only allowed to go to Cascina on market days or for church, and even then, only with a chaperone. "Well then, go already," she growled.

He smirked and swiped a few carrots from a basket. Then he nodded toward the chicken in her hands. "Someone's in a 'fowl' mood."

She raised the chicken to throw at him, and he ducked away, laughing.

By early afternoon Francesca couldn't sit still anymore. Despite her ankle and the specter of Signora Bianchi's wrath, she had to get up and move around. She excused herself, slipped a couple carrots into her pocket for Achilles, gathered her crutches, and hobbled out through the cavernous great hall filled with long tables and benches. Servants moved among the tables as they cleared up after the students' midday meal.

Besides serving as dining hall and occasional ballroom, the great hall was also used for fencing class in bad weather.

The eight-foot double doors stood open as usual as she passed into the marbled entry hall. Curved staircases descended to the floor on either side of her with hallways beyond them. The wing of the villa to her left made up most of the school—classrooms and offices on this floor, and sleeping quarters and common rooms for the students above.

The right wing held bedrooms for the teachers as well as public spaces, and family areas on the second floor.

Francesca crutched through the entry and out into the courtyard, toward the stable. If she couldn't ride Achilles with her injury, she could at least give him a good brushing. Besides, he always made her feel better.

Chaos and noise filled the courtyard. To her left, Papa worked with the most advanced fencers on technique with rapier and cape. Papa put one arm across Antonio's back and with his other hand, bent Antonio's blade hand inward as he explained some finer point to the gathered young men. Antonio nodded. Two Spaniards, Leandro and Rafael, tilted their heads and watched intently. Jealousy and loss seared through Francesca, and she looked away.

Other groups of students fenced with practice blades or rough-housed. A few sat reading or working on lessons. Two servant boys threw pebbles at a black cat backed against the stone wall. Francesca crutched toward them to rescue Shadow, but before she reached them, Catalina's brother, Enzo, scooped up the cat and chased the boys away.

"Thank you," Francesca called to Enzo. He smiled and tipped an imaginary hat to her as another student called to him.

A wooden *thunk* caught Francesca's attention. A dozen paces to her right, beneath the canvas awning of faded orange and white stripes, sat racks of gleaming steel practice foils and pine benches. One of the benches had tipped over. Next to it stood the golden-haired boy. He wore a white linen shirt, open at the throat, and a pair of dark blue breeches. His eyebrows were furrowed, and he held his palms out as if trying to calm two fellow students who stood in front of him, Burckhardt and Pietro.

Francesca crutched toward them. Perhaps the new pupil needed a rescue as well.

Burckhardt's hands were balled into fists and his mouth pulled into a frown. He was more than a head taller than Lord Worthington and nearly twice as wide, the largest student at the salle. *Strong but slow*, thought Francesca. *He intimidates the other students when they fence; that's how he wins so often, despite his lack of speed.*

Lord Worthington shook his head as he spoke to Pietro in English and motioned toward Burckhardt. "I don't understand. Why is he angry? Tell him I meant no offence."

Pietro smiled down his blade-thin nose, deepening the shadows under his cheekbones. *Pietro's quick with his blade, but he has poor point control.* He turned to Burckhardt and said in French, "He says that it's not his fault you are so ugly."

Francesca might have laughed, but she knew how thin-skinned Burckhardt was, seeing offenses even when none were meant. He constantly overreacted. A number of the students, like Pietro, made a sport of baiting him.

Burckhardt reached for Lord Worthington with one hand and cocked his other fist back. The young man backed away, tripped over the upturned bench, and fell to the cobblestones. Burckhardt bent over him.

"Lord Ernst!" Francesca called.

Burckhardt froze, but his stone-grey eyes turned to her—eyes too small for his wide brow and jaw.

"Pietro's lying. That's not what he said," she told him.

Pietro let out a protest, "I would never!"

Burckhardt straightened and let the punch fly—not at Lord Worthington on the ground, but into Pietro's gut. Pietro bent over with an "oof." Burckhardt hurried to Francesca, slicking back his ash-blond hair.

Francesca turned to crutch on toward the stables, annoyed as Burckhardt fell into step beside her. He was always nice enough to her, too attentive, but courteous. But he was so sensitive she could never relax around him. Burckhardt had challenged at least half a dozen students to duels with practice blades. And he sometimes treated the servants poorly. She couldn't abide that.

"Francesca, I'm sorry to see that you're injured. Is there any way I might be of assistance?" he asked.

"Thank you for your concern. I'm managing quite well." She glanced back toward the benches. Pietro had disappeared. Lord Worthington stood looking after them with a confused expression. She felt her cheeks flush. His fair skin and ruddy cheeks made his eyes unbelievably blue. She looked away.

"I should be more than happy to convey you wherever you need to go," Burckhardt said with an eager look.

Francesca could think of few things more appalling than being carried around by Burckhardt, but she gave him a polite smile. "You are too kind, but I'm sure you must have important things to attend to."

Burckhardt straightened. "As it happens, I'm currently unoccupied."

Francesca had reached the gate, so she stopped and turned to him. "No need, I'm only going to the stable. Good day, Lord Ernst." She hoped he'd take the hint.

He didn't. "Then I'll accompany you. I may be of use to you there."

"It's quite unnecessary," she said trying to hold her irritation in check.

"But I insist." Burckhardt moved closer to her. "It would be very ungallant of me to leave you unattended."

Francesca took a breath and tried to relax her jaw muscles before she said what was on her mind; that it was even more ungallant to force his company on her. He was certain to be offended if she said that.

Luckily, Enzo approached.

"Excuse me. I hope I'm not intruding, but I could use Lord Ernst's help."

My hero, thought Francesca, stifling a sigh of relief.

Burckhardt looked annoyed, but asked, "How may I be of assistance?"

"You have such an excellent line on your *mezzo cerchio* parry, I wondered if you might demonstrate for me," Enzo said.

Francesca hid a smile. Burckhardt was no better than Enzo at low-line parries. Most likely, Enzo was coming to her rescue.

Burckhardt's chest seemed to puff up an inch or two. He turned to Francesca. "If you're quite sure you don't need me."

"Thank you, but it appears you're needed more elsewhere," she said.

Burckhardt gave her a bow, wished her a speedy recovery, and headed back toward the salle.

Before he turned away, Enzo gave her a wink, which Francesca answered with a grin.

Earthy smells of hay and horse enveloped her as she entered the coolness of the stone stable. The double row of dark wood stalls could house thirty horses in a pinch, though there were seldom more than fifteen or so in residence. A groom stopped and touched his hat as he pushed a barrow full of pungent manure past her and out the door. Another groom, six stalls down, bridled a bay horse.

Francesca's stomach tightened as she passed the spot on the floor where she'd failed so miserably against Sebi last night.

When she entered Achilles' stall, he tossed his head in greeting. She put an arm around his neck, but not even Achilles could take away the sting of last night. Her shoulders hunched against the weight of her disappointment. She barely held back tears as memories of her seventh birthday flooded back.

With a flurry of anticipation, she had rushed down the stairs to breakfast. She was sure what her gift from Papa would be—what she wanted more than anything in the world.

Papa wasn't there when she arrived breathless, but Nana stood near the fire leaning on her cane. She opened her arms and Francesca rushed in.

"There's my sweet girl. Happy birthday." Nana gave Francesca a hug. She nodded to a bundle on the table. "Something to go with your beautiful green eyes."

Francesca held up a lovely emerald velvet dress embroidered with silver butterflies. "Oh, Nana! It's wonderful. When did you have time to do this?"

"Oh, a little here, a little there." She smiled.

Antonio and Sebi appeared and spooned eggs from a silver ewer onto plates at the sideboard as they wished her a happy birthday. When she heard Papa's footsteps in the hall, her heart thumped.

Papa entered with his hands behind his back. "There's my brave girl, seven years old and nearly grown." He strode toward her.

His smile didn't reach his eyes. He was always a little sad on her birthday since it also marked the day her mother had died. He bent and kissed her on the top of her head. Francesca's breath caught as with a flourish he presented her gift.

A china doll.

Disappointment knocked the breath from her. It was a beautiful doll, made to look like her with auburn hair, green eyes, and a dress to match the one Nana had given her, but she hated it with all her heart.

She burst into tears as she ran from the room. With bleary eyes she bolted up the stairs, slammed her door, and threw herself on her bed. She sobbed into her pillow. She had been so sure that this was the year.

On their sixth birthdays both Antonio and Sebi had received beautifully engraved rapiers that bore their names and the DiCesare coat of arms. Those gifts had marked the beginning of their formal fencing training.

On her sixth birthday Papa had given her a silver locket, engraved with the DiCesare coat of arms, that contained an auburn curl of her mother's hair. Francesca loved the gift but couldn't stop her disappointment. At least a hundred times in the next year she had asked Papa if she could start her training. Papa would shake his head and say "No, my Cesca," then send her off to Nana or her governess.

Her seventh birthday was supposed to be different. She reasoned that perhaps girls needed another year to grow before they could learn to fence. There were no other girls at the salle except servants so she had little to judge by, but surely her lessons must start eventually. After all, Nana had once mentioned that Papa had taught her mother to fence. Today was supposed to be the day she received her sword and started her training.

She heard Papa's footsteps in the hall and a knock on her door. "Cesca?"

She didn't answer, but he came in and sat down next to her on the bed. He sighed heavily. She didn't look at him.

"I know what you were hoping for," he said. "I'm truly sorry, dear heart, but I can't give you what you want. I won't. Girls don't fence."

"But. Nana said that Mamma—"

"It was a mistake. I won't make it again. No."

Francesca gulped air between sobs. He put a warm hand on her back. His voice sounded weary.

"I've seen too much in this world, Francesca. Men are brutish, hard. Women, girls are meant for higher things. You are the best of us. You have a beautiful life ahead of you, Cesca. But it cannot include the sword."

He turned her gently to look at him. "It breaks my heart to deny you, but I must. So you must stop asking. I forbid you to ask me again." He kissed her cheek, then rose, and left her with her tears.

That was the day she stole a discarded practice blade and began lessons in her room. Over nine years ago now.

Achilles' nickering brought her back to the present. "And the next day he brought me you," she told him as she stroked his neck, as black and glistening as onyx, but soft as a breath. "Buying back my affection, no doubt." He nibbled at her pocket and she pulled out the carrots. As he munched, she set her crutches aside, took up a brush, and held on to him with one arm as she worked the tangles out of his mane. She shook her head. "It's not fair—"

"Miss DiCesare?" someone said in English.

She turned and froze in place. It was him.

"Are you Miss DiCesare?" he asked again.

Francesca realized she'd been staring without saying a word. She'd never seen eyes that deep aqua color, or such perfect lips with delightful dimples at the corners. Heat washed her face, and she knew she was blushing.

She was suddenly conscious of how plain she was, how sweaty from the cookfire, how pathetic she must have looked on her crutches, and how much soot smudged her hands. She tried to say something, but nothing came out. She turned back to Achilles as she nodded and watched him from the corner of her eye. She brushed Achilles' neck as more sweat gathered in her armpits.

"Well, I, I know this is irregular. I don't mean to presume. I don't know if you speak English, but I wanted to thank you. I think you saved me from a walloping."

She glanced at him. "You're welcome."

His whole body seemed to relax at her words. He ran a hand through his burnished hair. "Thank God, you do speak English. I'm Phillip Worthington. I'm glad to make your acquaintance."

She gave a small curtsy. "Welcome to Salle DiCesare, Lord Worthington."

He smiled and she had to look away or she'd be tongue-tied again.

"Please, call me Phillip," he said. "I was hoping you could tell me what happened back there?"

Francesca laughed and relaxed just a little. "The big fellow is Lord Burckhardt Ernst. He's related to the King of Prussia and likes everyone to know it."

"And why, pray, did the King of Prussia's relative wish to beat my brains in?"

Francesca gave a nervous giggle. "You need to find a more reliable interpreter."

"Ah," Phillip said. "I suspected the thin fellow was *embellishing* my words."

"Pietro Balsamo, son of the richest merchant in Naples. His hobby is starting fights, particularly between nobles. I think he enjoys seeing them injure one another."

"Wonderful," Phillip said, moving around the stall. "Any suggestions as to what I might do about it?" He reached toward Achilles. Francesca moved to intervene since Achilles was not fond of strangers, but to her surprise Achilles let him scratch his jowls.

Francesca shrugged. "You could challenge Pietro to a duel."

Phillip frowned. "That seems excessive. I've no wish to hurt him. And wouldn't that land me in trouble?"

She shook her head. "Not as long as you follow the rules of proper dueling. And you're only allowed to use practice blades."

"I see." Phillip rubbed his chin. "And that would stop this Balsamo from causing trouble for me?"

Francesca tilted her head to one side. "Perhaps," she replied, thoughtfully, "if you beat him soundly. But Pietro's not bad. And you'd have to find two people willing to act as your seconds in the duel."

Phillip grimaced. "That might be difficult. Does anyone else speak English?"

"My family and one or two others. But certainly, you must speak French. Everyone speaks French nowadays."

"My education at home was … lacking. My footman does."

"Is he going to do your lessons? Classes are in French and Italian."

Phillip let out a sigh that deflated his chest, and Francesca felt a twinge of pity.

"I'm sure Signor Gallo will help you," she said, to boost his spirits.

"He's the schoolmaster?"

"Yes, but everyone calls him La Tartaruga, the Turtle."

"Why?"

Francesca smiled. "You'll see."

Phillip patted her horse. "He's a handsome lad. What's his name?"

"Achilles."

Phillip laughed, nodding toward the small patch of white on Achilles' right hock—the only light spot on his jet-black coat. "Of course, that must be his Achilles' heel."

Francesca grinned and nodded.

"Do you ride?" asked Phillip.

"Whenever I can," Francesca said, indicating her crutches.

"That's my Belgian, Iago." Phillip pointed four stalls down to his white horse. Iago tossed his head at the sound of his name.

Francesca chuckled. "Iago? Like Shakespeare's villain?"

Phillip gave her another devastating smile. "Precisely. He'd as soon throw you as look at you. He should never be trusted, but I do anyway." He paused. "Perhaps we could go for a ride once you're healed. It would be a pleasure to have someone to talk to."

Francesca's heart pounded. She had to turn back to Achilles before she could stutter, "I, I'd like that." Of course, Signora Bianchi would never allow it, but Papa might. "If I may."

"I'll look forward to it," Phillip said.

Francesca set aside the curry brush and took up her crutches. It was high time she get back to the kitchen. Phillip opened the stall door for her, and she crutched out of the stable with him.

As they passed the corner of the stable Francesca pointed with her chin back behind the building where a one-hundred-foot elm towered over a patch of well-trodden earth. "Those are the dueling grounds."

He nodded, thoughtful. "Perhaps I would be wise to size up Balsamo's skill before I issue any challenges. I imagine losing would put me in an even worse position."

"Most likely," agreed Francesca. She spotted her governess across the courtyard and stopped outside the gate. She didn't want to be seen or she'd get a lecture for leaving the kitchen.

Phillip seemed to take that as his cue. He gave her a graceful bow. "Thank you again for the rescue. And the advice was most useful."

"I'm glad," Francesca replied. "Good luck."

He smiled and turned toward the crowded courtyard. "Once more unto the breach, dear friends," he pronounced as he plunged into the throng.

Francesca laughed as she headed back into the stable to wait until Signora Bianchi went inside. How exciting to find someone else who read Shakespeare! Most of the students would rather have their eyes gouged out. But then, none of them were English.

Phillip rejoining his fellow students wasn't quite the same as King Henry invading Harfleur, but she supposed it did require some bravery.

Bravery.

Her words to Sebi last night came back to her. *I'm plenty brave enough to fence.* She stopped outside Achilles' stall and looked into his soft black eye and saw her own reflection. "I wasn't afraid. Not at all. I am brave enough." Sebi had said that real fencing wasn't doing the footwork and blade work, it was having the courage. Well, she'd proven that.

Achilles nickered back.

"Maybe I could fence. Maybe it's not impossible if I had some practice with an actual opponent. I was too eager, not too frightened."

A weight lifted from her but then crashed down again. Who could she possibly fence with? *Sebi will never agree after last night, and none of the others can be trusted with my secret.* She leaned her forehead against Achilles' cheek. "I wish you could fence with me."

After a few minutes she headed back to the courtyard. The signora was nowhere in sight, so she went on toward the kitchen to take her seat by the fire. As she crutched through the great hall, a thought hit her and jerked her to a stop.

The thought was perfectly delicious and terribly naughty. Best of all, it meant she would get to spend time with Phillip. But first she'd have to convince Papa to let her go riding with him.

CHAPTER 4
A SLIGHT CHANCE

Francesca knew that Signora Bianchi would never—even if her life depended upon it—give her permission to ride with Phillip. Such things were scandalous. But Papa was not so easily scandalized.

She waited until Friday, when Papa was distracted by the week's correspondence, to broach the subject. By then she was off the crutches.

After she finished kitchen duty, she knocked on the door to his office with one hand as she balanced a tea tray in the other.

"Come in," he called.

Golden late-afternoon sun slanted in from the garden window, lighting the lustrous dark-wood paneling. Dust motes circled in the beams. Papa sat at his rosewood desk, quill in one hand, the other hand cupping his graying goatee. His steel eyes stared into the distance, lost in thought, his brows drawn down, but he smiled when he saw her.

"Would you like some tea, Papa?"

"Thank you, Cesca."

He picked up a letter as Francesca set down the tray. "It's past time I made another trip through France and England. There are urgent matters that need my attention and I've stayed away too long."

Francesca gripped the handle tight as she poured the tea and forgot about her carefully laid plan for a moment. "I hate when you go away. Travel is so dangerous. I worry."

Every few years he traveled across Europe teaching signature moves to noble houses, giving fencing demonstrations, and recruiting students for the salle. But the seas were full of pirates and the land full of bandits. Not even Papa's sword arm could save him from a highwayman's bullet.

Papa leaned forward and put his hand over hers for a moment. "Leave the worrying to me. I'll do enough for us both."

She gave him a small smile. "I'll try."

"I'm tempted to take Antonio with me, but he'll be needed here to work with the younger students. Maybe next time, when Sebastian is older."

Francesca suppressed a spike of jealousy knowing he would never take her along.

One point of the journey was to reach England. That was where he had married Francesca's mother. Some of her family remained there, though Francesca had never met them. It was to honor her mother that Papa had insisted that she and her brothers learn to speak English well.

The other reason to go to England was Billy, a boy that Papa had fostered since before she was born. He would be twenty now, a grown man. Papa wrote to Billy every month and always seemed melancholy or wistful afterwards, his thoughts more of the past than the present.

"Must you go?" Francesca said.

"You mustn't begrudge Billy a few months of my time," Papa said. "The boy is family in—"

"—all but blood, I know," Francesca finished for him. She wondered why Papa never answered questions as to how he had become "family."

"Yes, well, he's chosen a dangerous course, and I must stop him if I can." Papa picked up a paper in front of him and rubbed the back of his neck. "I pray that I'm not too late."

Billy was nothing to her but a name she resented because he took Papa away. She had more pressing matters to wrangle.

"Speaking of English boys." She paused and tried to relax the tension in her shoulders. There was a good chance her ploy would backfire, but she took the plunge anyway. "I was hoping you might forbid me to ride with Lord Worthington."

"You want … what?" Papa asked.

"I understand that he's homesick and that few people here speak his language, but why should *I* have to entertain him. I thought, well, if you forbid me, then I won't appear cruel when I tell him no."

"He has asked you to go riding?" He rolled up the paper in his hands.

"Yes, Papa. I translated for him, and he said how relieved he was to have someone to talk to, but I have my lessons to do and kitchen duties, and signora wants me to help inventory the silverware. Why must I be the one to make him feel welcome?"

Papa frowned. "Because you're the lady of the house. We all must make him feel at home here." He smoothed down his goatee with his fingers. "I had assumed he at least spoke French. Everyone speaks French."

"That's what I thought."

"I didn't realize the boy was having so much trouble."

Francesca shrugged. "Lord Worthington's too proud to tell you, and he could hardly admit as much to Sebastian or Antonio. You know how they would tease him."

"Lads can be harsh. I'll have to speak with them and with Signor Gallo to see what's to be done." He pushed back his chair and rose.

"So I'm forbidden to ride with him, aren't I?" She tried to sound hopeful.

"Under the circumstances I think a ride is little enough to ask."

"But Papa!"

She pretended to sulk as she left the room, struggling to hide her excitement.

Francesca spotted Phillip coming into the great hall for dinner and arranged to meet him in the stable shortly after daybreak the following morning—early enough that her governess wouldn't look for her for at least an hour.

Francesca was nervous, partly about riding with Phillip, but mostly about her next plan. He needed to learn either Italian or French and she needed to fence. It seemed only logical that they help each other, but she would have to convince him of that.

Phillip slipped the bridle over Iago's head as she entered the stable.

"Buon giorno," Phillip greeted her with a smile. He was wearing a grey frock coat with a black velvet collar and pale grey breeches. Shadows under both his eyes showed he was tired, though on his right side the shadow circled his azure eye in a blue-green smudge.

Francesca had heard at dinner that the black eye was the result of a fight Pietro had manufactured between Phillip and two Spanish lads. Papa had disciplined Pietro after he'd questioned the Spaniards, but the damage was done.

Francesca felt sorry for Phillip and returned his smile. "Good morning to you too," she said in English. "Apparently your Italian is coming along."

Phillip shook his head. "After a week all I can manage is please, thank you, good morning, and good evening."

"Well, that's better than last week."

"Much better." Phillip rolled his eyes. "Now I can *thank* the other students for the beatings."

Francesca chuckled. She threw a saddle blanket over Achilles' back as Cassio, the head groom, brought over her sidesaddle.

Cassio's white hair contrasted sharply with his tanned, lined face. The wrinkles that gathered at the corners of his eyes and mouth accentuated his tendency to smile and laugh. The smell of fresh hay wafted from him as he hefted Francesca's sidesaddle onto Achilles and tightened the girth.

Phillip glanced around the stable. "Hadn't we better bring someone with us?" he asked. "I wouldn't want to … cause you any trouble."

Francesca chaffed at the necessity and had thought seriously about who to bring. She knew propriety demanded a chaperone, but she wanted someone who wouldn't listen in on their conversation. Catalina didn't speak English, but she could tell at a glance when Francesca was up to something. Her brothers would eaves drop, and the maids would gossip no end.

"Of course," she said as she turned to Cassio. "Is Mateo ready?"

Cassio nodded, amusement dancing in his eyes, just as it had when she'd gone over this with him last night. "Mateo!"

Mateo stuck his head out of the last stall.

"Yes, sir?" He was about thirteen years old, with shoulder-length, unruly hair, and large dark eyes. Francesca knew he didn't speak a word of English, so they'd still be able to talk privately, sort of.

"Time to go," Cassio said.

"Yes, sir." Mateo limped toward them. He'd been kicked by a horse last year. Francesca and Signora Bianchi had set and plastered the leg, but it hadn't healed quite right. He led Reginia, the oldest and slowest horse in the stable.

Cassio winked at her. "The old girl's ready, just as you asked, mistress."

Francesca broke into a smile. At least Cassio was on her side. Now she was sure to get some time alone with Phillip.

Francesca thanked him as she and Phillip led their horses out into the yard.

Her smile quirked to one side. "Next time someone is angry with you, tell them: *Pietro detto, non a me.*"

Phillip repeated the phrase. "What does that mean?"

"It means: Pietro said it, not me."

Phillip laughed. "That just might work."

Cassio led Reginia out with Mateo on her back. Then he gave Francesca a leg up into her sidesaddle. Phillip swung up onto Iago's back and they headed out.

A gray sky hung low, robbing the landscape of color. Mist nestled in the valleys and made an island of each of the surrounding hills. They headed east, past the barn and sheep pastures toward the vineyard beyond.

Phillip's grey and black riding jacket contrasted crisply against Iago's white coat. The chill air reddened Phillip's cheeks and stung hers. He glanced back at Mateo and the plodding Reginia, who had already fallen behind, then turned to her.

"*Pietro detto, non a me* is the most useful thing I've learned all week," Phillip said. "Do you have any other helpful phrases you can teach me?"

"You can always try: *Non è colpa mia,*" Francesca said. "It's not my fault. Or *Non era me*, it wasn't me."

Phillip grinned. "You're a much better teacher than Signor Gallo. I don't suppose you might be willing to tutor me."

A thrill lodged in Francesca's chest, but then she became suspicious. This was going too well. Things were never that easy. Calm, she thought and let out a breath. She needed to act as though she were doing him a favor.

"That's not fair to Signor Gallo; he's a brilliant man."

Phillip scrunched up his face. "Perhaps, but so far, it's not going very well. I can't understand half of what he says. You speak much better English."

"*Grazie,*" Francesca said. "But—"

"I don't mean alone, of course. I don't want to cause you any trouble." He glanced back at Mateo lagging behind them.

Francesca hesitated, unsure how to broach the whole object of this ride.

Sensing her hesitation, Phillip hurried on. "I realize your time is valuable. I don't mean to suggest you have nothing better to do than help such an inept student. We could make a business deal of sorts if it would help. I could arrange some sort of recompense." His hand went to a leather pouch that hung at his side.

"I don't want your money!" She glanced back at Mateo who gave her an uncomfortable smile.

Phillip's face fell. "My apologies. I meant no insult. I know it's a good deal to ask of you, but I, I need your help. I can't trust any of the others not to switch the words around. I'll end up wishing folks a pleasant hippopotamus or something."

Francesca smiled as her heart beat loudly. She patted Achilles and squeezed the reins tight to keep her hands from shaking.

She tasted fear at the back of her throat. If Phillip told, she'd never get another chance. She dropped her voice, even though she knew Mateo wouldn't understand. "What I want, is for you to fence with me."

Phillip laughed. "Now you're making fun of me too."

The laughter stung, but it was better than disdain. "No, I'm quite serious."

"Why would *you* want to fence?"

She covered the annoyance that shot through her with a smile. "What difference does it make?"

Phillip shrugged. "I've never met a girl who wanted to fence. Perhaps Italian women fence all the time, but women don't where I come from."

Francesca glanced at him, heartened that he would even consider the possibility that women fenced somewhere.

They had slowed their pace and Mateo had caught up to them. Francesca tried to act nonchalant, as though they were just making small talk. "Nor do they here. It's just … me. Will you help me?"

Phillip shot a look at Mateo, and the boy squirmed uncomfortably. "Your father is the best sword master in the country. Since you're asking me, not him, I gather it's against the rules. I'd like to help, but I can't. I don't want to cause trouble."

Francesca dropped her voice again. "If we're caught, I'll be the one punished. Not you."

Phillip gave her a crooked frown. "I'm sure there would be enough punishment to go around."

"Fine." Francesca spurred Achilles on, hoping for a little distance from their chaperone. "I'm sure The Turtle won't mind teaching you indefinitely. It's unfortunate about his breath, but I imagine you'll get used to it."

Phillip nudged Iago to canter up alongside. "There must be something else that you want. Sweets perhaps, or some nice tortoise-shell combs for your hair. I could get you fine fabrics from England for dresses."

"No, *grazie*. Papa will buy me all the sweets and baubles I want. I don't give a cat's whisker for such things."

"There must be something, surely."

"There's only one thing I've ever wanted, and you already know what it is." She couldn't bear saying the words out loud again.

"Why ask me?"

Francesca reined in Achilles, and Phillip stopped next to her. She spoke quickly, before Mateo joined them. "Because I can't trust anyone else either. If they tell, if Papa finds out, I'll, I'll be sent away."

"It's a good bet I would be too." Phillip shook his head. "Why would you take that risk? Why would you want me to?"

She looked forward so Mateo wouldn't see her face. "Because, because I have to." The words sounded childish to her, but she could think of no others. Perhaps she was being selfish asking him to risk expulsion. But there was no one else.

He was quiet a moment, then said, "There's something I *must* do as well, something that requires me to remain here. I'm sorry."

Reginia had caught up again, so they turned west and rode in silence down a row of the vineyard that was just beginning to leaf out in dots of pale green among tangled walls of gray vines. Francesca felt as if those vines were growing and knotting together to form a gray cage that would keep her locked up in a dull world forever. She had to break free, and she needed Phillip to do it.

She couldn't give up yet. She still had a few cards to play. "You know you have to earn your place in a fencing competition."

She suppressed a shiver as she remembered how close Catalina had come to being sent home with Enzo.

Phillip nodded.

"Did you also know that no matter how well you fence, if you fail your studies, you'll be sent home?"

Phillip didn't respond.

When she glanced at him, he was chewing on his lower lip. She felt guilty. Everything was stacked against him. She wanted to help him and knew she was being unfair, but what about her? As a nobleman's son, Phillip would have a lifetime of freedom. He could travel, learn what he wished, do as he wished for as long as he wished. All she wanted was this one shining thing in a life that would be stuck in one place, filled up with balancing dreary household accounts, managing servants, and minding children.

"I'd like to help you, too," she said, finally. "But all I've ever wanted was to fence. I've practiced every day since I was little." She paused to steady her quavering voice. She hurried Achilles to put a little distance between them and Mateo again. "I've read every book. I've watched and listened, and thought about fencing day in, day out, year after year, but…" She hesitated as her throat tightened. "But, I've never fenced." She took a deep breath. "I have to, and you have to help me."

"I would," he started. Then the muscles in his face and hands tightened. His blue eyes darkened as they narrowed, and he looked away down the row of vines. Francesca was taken aback by a sudden savageness in his expression. "But I need justice. There's someone I must challenge to a duel—someone I need to defeat." His voice was sharp. "And he's very good, so I have to be better." Then just as suddenly the expression disappeared. His features relaxed and he turned back to her. "I have to stay here and learn. I can't risk that."

Francesca's thoughts whirled. This was a Phillip she hadn't expected—a man on a quest like some knight of old, one who was haunted and intriguing, a puzzle for her to solve. She wanted more than ever to spend time with him. Who could he want to duel so badly that he'd travel all the way across Europe and spend years learning how? Who could he hate enough to be willing to risk death to defeat him? Who did he need justice for?

She remained quiet, hoping he'd say more.

When he didn't, she pointed out the flaw in his plan. "But you can't stay here and learn unless you speak Italian."

Phillip eyebrows furrowed.

They rode on in silence.

The sun peeked through the clouds just as the threesome left the grapevines, crossed the rutted dirt road leading to the salle, and headed into the olive grove. The evenly spaced, gnarled tree trunks squiggled upward into a silver-green canopy. A breeze ruffled the leaves setting them whispering.

They were at an impasse. Much as Francesca wanted to spend time figuring him out, she wanted to fence more. Feeling her chance slipping away, she racked her brain for a way to push him to agree. She guessed that his mind was running through the other people at the salle that he could ask for help. That's what she'd be doing in his place. He might conclude that it was safer to trust Sebi or Antonio, then she'd lose her chance for good.

She reined up again and Reginia, just behind her, nearly ran into Achilles.

"*Scusi*," Mateo apologized. He directed Reginia around Achilles, and the old girl plodded off a few paces.

"Look," Francesca said to Phillip. "Either way, one of us is going to be unhappy. I'll give you a fifty-fifty chance at having it your way."

Phillip narrowed his eyes. "What do you mean?"

"I'll race you for it," Francesca said.

Phillip's eyebrows shot up. "What precisely is *it*?"

"If you win," Francesca said, "I'll help you with your Italian lessons. If I win, I'll help you with Italian and you fence with me."

Phillip rubbed his face as his eyes traveled over Achilles, sizing him up.

Iago was more muscular than Achilles, broader through the chest and haunches and taller, which meant he had a longer stride.

"Are you certain? I like my chances," Phillip said.

Francesca shrugged. "Better a slim chance than none."

A smile swept slowly across his face. Was that a touch of admiration she saw in his eyes?

"Deal," he said.

There it was. She had another chance. She held out her hand and they shook. Phillip's hand was harder and more callused than she expected for a nobleman's son, and her palm tingled when he let go.

"Come on, Mateo," Francesca said as they rode down the row of trees. "We're going to race."

"Race, mistress?" Mateo asked. "This old girl would rather sleep than race."

"It will be good for her," Francesca said. "She can sleep the rest of the day."

They emerged into a pasture, then turned their horses to face back down the shadowed row they had just traveled. Lines of dark trunks stretched forward on each side of them for one hundred yards. Reginia cropped at some weeds as Francesca pointed down the grassy lane between the olive trees. "We race around the far end of this row," she indicated the line of trees on their left, "and back here. The edge of the grove is the finish line."

"Agreed," Phillip said as they maneuvered their horses into position.

Francesca repeated the rules in Italian for Mateo, and he nodded.

"On three," Francesca said. "*Uno.*"

Phillip nodded. At least he knew that much Italian.

Francesca's heart felt ready to catapult from her chest. That wonderful, familiar fire seared through her veins.

"*Due.*"

She would win this. She had to. She squeezed her right knee around the pommel of her sidesaddle and gathered the reins tighter.

"*Tre!*"

She clapped her left heel to Achilles' side and pushed forward with her hands. "Go!" she cried to Achilles. He leapt forward. His muscles strained, but Phillip and Iago were right alongside.

"Run!" she shouted as she bent over her thigh along Achilles' back. He stretched into his stride. The pounding of his hooves drummed up her spine, wind ripping at her hair.

As Iago pulled slightly ahead, Francesca tightened every muscle. She propelled Achilles forward with force of will. They flew down the track, dark tree trunks flashing by.

The light at the far end of the grove grew brighter as Achilles, muscles straining, pulled ahead. She shot a look at Phillip and Iago.

Phillip hunched over Iago's neck. Iago's forelegs pumped the ground and his nostrils flared.

Francesca's heart soared. She would win! They were half a length ahead and she could hear the harsh rasp of Iago's breathing.

They reached the end of the row, Phillip on the inside track. As Achilles, the nimbler horse, cut the corner close, Iago ran full into Achilles' thigh.

Francesca grabbed handfuls of mane and held on. Her stomach lurched as the grove slewed around her. Achilles spun and nearly fell. Somehow, he kept his legs under him, running wide.

Francesca's heart pounded. Ahead of them, Iago and Phillip thundered toward the finish line. *No! I can't lose! I won't!*

She clapped her heel to Achilles' side again. "Come on, Achilles! Let's beat him!"

They flew down the lane of trees, following Phillip and Iago. Patches of sunlight flashed by. Francesca urged Achilles on, pushing forward with each stride. Achilles shook his head, gathered his haunches, and sprinted faster. His ribs heaved against her calves. As they pulled closer, Francesca crouched lower, squinting into the wind, her blood pounding through her veins.

As they neared the finish, Achilles and she came alongside Iago and Phillip.

Francesca caught a glimpse of astonishment on Phillip's face as they blew past. They burst out of the grove, into the brightness of the pasture a neck ahead.

As she reined Achilles in, laughter bubbled through her and burst out into the morning air. Achilles snorted and shook his head. She looked over at Phillip as a different kind of warmth spread through her. His golden hair was tousled by the wind, his cheeks glowed red, and his eyes sparkled.

"Best two out of three?" he said.

Achilles and Iago panted for breath as their sides heaved.

Francesca shook her head as she scratched Achilles behind the ear. "It would be cruel of me to prolong your suffering. We'd just beat you again."

Phillip patted Iago's shoulder. "Iago's fast, but Achilles flies."

Francesca nodded, catching her own breath. She looked back down the track. Mateo and Reginia had just made the turn. She laughed again.

"Well look," Phillip said, flushing a deeper red. "I'm sorry…"

A spear of fear went through her. He was going to back out of their bargain. "You needn't apologize for running into us," Francesca hurried to say. "I'm just so glad that you're a gentleman and a man of honor, who would never go back on his word."

Phillip pressed his lips into a line for a moment, then he shrugged. "Indeed."

Francesca felt aglow with happiness. Finally, she would have a real person to fence with *and* she would get to spend time with Phillip. Perfect.

Now she just needed to figure out where and when.

CHAPTER 5
SISTERS

As Francesca and Phillip cantered toward the stable, they planned for Francesca to join Phillip's next tutoring session with Signor Gallo that evening. Though Francesca had agreed to teach Phillip, they needed The Turtle to agree as well.

As they approached the stable, Cassio came out to meet them—followed by Signora Bianchi. Judging by the signora's red, mottled face and her eyebrows pinched together at her beak of a nose, Francesca was in deep trouble. Usually that would have sent dread through her, but today she nearly laughed out loud. She was too happy to care. Today was her birthday and Christmas rolled into one.

Francesca slid from the saddle without waiting for Cassio to help her.

"For goodness' sake, Francesca! What could possibly have possessed you to go riding alone with a strange man?" The signora narrowed her eyes at Phillip as if trying to assess what horrific crime he had intended.

"I wasn't alone," Francesca said. "We brought Mateo."

The signora huffed. "Mateo? You felt *he* was an appropriate chaperone? Where is he?"

"He'll be along. He's just behind us," Francesca said as Phillip swung out of the saddle.

He bowed gallantly to Signora Bianchi. "*Buon giorno, signora.*"

She squeezed her eyes closed a moment and expelled her breath.

"Young man, you should know better than to leave your chaperone behind and risk tarnishing a young woman's reputation."

Francesca's cheeks flamed. "No tarnishing occurred, signora," Francesca said. "And anyway, he doesn't speak Italian."

"You are not the one who decides if tarnishing has occurred. It is decided by public opinion, and often against your will." With a tight curtsy, she motioned for Phillip to continue into the stable. He shot Francesca a sympathetic look as he led Iago away.

Mateo appeared from the olive grove walking Reginia. The two limped along together.

The Signora continued. "I shall speak to your father about your behavior."

"Please do," Francesca said confidently. "He ordered me to ride with Lord Worthington to make him feel welcome."

Signora Bianchi looked heavenward for a moment. "And I suppose he ordered you to bring Mateo on that nag. Honestly, Francesca. You must consider propriety. I'm at my wit's end. Why must I continually save you from yourself?"

Francesca bit back the retort on her lips. What did it matter who chaperoned? Why would anyone besides the signora care? She hadn't asked to be saved.

She pulled the reins over Achilles' head more forcefully than she'd intended and led him toward Cassio who stood at a respectful distance. He too gave her a sympathetic look as she handed him the reins.

Francesca knew young ladies were supposed to be modest, proper, and agreeable. Well, try as she might, she was none of those things. Pretending might catch her a husband, but a husband who expected her to be meek would be sorely disappointed. What was the good in that?

"We shall deal with this later," Signora Bianchi declared as she herded Francesca toward the salle. "We have visitors."

"Who?" asked Francesca. She forgot her flash of anger and straightened her disheveled hair.

"The Aquinos have arrived."

Francesca clapped her hands together. The Aquinos were Catalina's parents. Francesca couldn't wait to see Signora Aquino. Never having known her mother, Francesca liked to imagine that she had been just like Signora Aquino. Same warm smile and kind eyes, with a willowy, curvaceous figure-except with cinnamon-colored hair and green eyes like her mother's portrait over the fireplace in the dining room.

Signora Bianchi ushered Francesca into the house and up the stairs to the old nursery. A pang of sadness greeted Francesca as she entered her old playroom. She remembered the hours she'd spent there with Nana reading to her or watching over her as she played.

Now Catalina bent over the old oak crib where her one-year-old brother sat waving plump arms. Catalina cooed at the child. Francesca couldn't remember the boy's name. She scanned the room. "Good morning, Catalina," she said, "Where is your mother? I heard she'd arrived."

"You just missed her. She and Father are speaking with the maestro. We'll see them later."

Francesca tried to hide her disappointment.

Catalina smiled as the child grabbed her finger and stuck it in his mouth. She turned to Francesca. "You'll have to manage the bookkeeping without me. I guess I'll be occupied this morning."

"Francesca will be helping you," Signora Bianchi said.

"Me!" Francesca said. She wasn't sure which was worse, going over the kitchen accounts or babysitting. And she didn't want to be stuck in the nursery when there were guests. She hoped to find Signora Aquino and say hello. Besides, she needed to find a place where she and Phillip could fence.

"I couldn't possibly impose," Catalina said.

Hope spiked and Francesca wanted to hug her. "As lady of the house, oughtn't I welcome our guests?" Francesca added.

"You should have been there to welcome them when they arrived. Instead, you were—" The signora frowned and glanced at Catalina. "Now you'll just have to wait until they've finished their conference. And frankly, you've spent precious little time with children. You could use the experience." She crossed to Catalina. "I trust you can handle this."

"Of course, signora," Catalina said.

Signora Bianchi lifted the baby onto her hip and returned to Francesca, who stood near the door eyeing the child.

"I expect you to make yourself useful," Signora Bianchi said as she pressed the baby boy into Francesca's arms.

"Yes, signora." Francesca braced against the doorway. He was heavier than he looked.

The signora left, still clearly annoyed.

"I'm so sorry you're stuck with us, mistress." Catalina said. "I know how much you like children."

Francesca shot her a look for the "mistress" and then shrugged and gave her a half smile. "At least we're together and not working out sums in the accounts book."

Catalina grinned.

A worn floral sofa and overstuffed armchair sat under the sunny windows at the far end of the room. Next to the crib stood a bookcase full of games and toys. The room hadn't been used in ages so there was a hint of mustiness in the air.

Benito. That was the little boy's name, Francesca remembered. They called him Beni. He was awkward to hold as he stretched backward and threw his head around. Francesca crossed the room, sank into the armchair, and bounced the struggling child on her knee.

Catalina scanned the collection of toys and games on the shelves for older children and frowned. She turned to Francesca. "I think I've got an old rag doll in my room. Can you watch him for a few moments?"

"I'm sure I can manage."

"I'll be right back." Catalina hurried out.

"Looks like it's just us," Francesca said to Beni.

His head swiveled around to look at her, his honey-brown eyes wide. Dark curls surrounded his face. He reached a plump hand out and grabbed her cheek. His fingers were hot and slimy.

Francesca forced a smile as she turned her head and wiped her cheek with her sleeve.

There were four children under three years old living at the salle. She'd seen how the other girls her age—Catalina, the three parlor maids, the cook's maids, and the two girls from the dairy—were drawn to the toddlers; the way they lit up with happiness when the little ones ran into their arms. Francesca wished she felt that way too. She knew everyone expected her to be happy, so she tried, but it always seemed unnatural.

She remembered the day Papa brought Achilles home. He had been a gangly, unsteady young colt, barely weaned. She loved him in an instant. Her heart had swelled to bursting when she wrapped her arms around him. She imagined that was the way other girls felt around children. That was certainly how it looked. Why didn't she?

She hugged Beni and he gummed her cheek and gurgled. *Eww.* She waited for some maternal longing, some surge of affection, but she felt only the heat of his body making her sweat where he pressed against her.

When he started to squirm, she set him down on the floor and let him crawl across the rug.

She looked around the room. Would the nursery work as a place for her and Phillip to fence? No one went there most of the time, but there were the windows to consider. The night watchman would notice a light inside and might investigate.

Shouts and laughter brought her attention to the window. Below, Sebi and a pack of his friends ran past, headed for the gardens. Francesca clenched her jaw. Beni grabbed her knee and hauled himself to his wobbly feet. "Look at you," she said acidly. "You'll be running and fencing in no time. And no one will say you can't."

Francesca thought of the night she fenced with Sebi. For a one-time bout the stable had worked fine, but long term, she and Phillip would eventually be caught—unless they spent most of their time watching instead of fencing.

Beni sat down hard on his bottom and burbled up a chinful of off-white goo. Francesca wrinkled her nose at the sour smell, then looked around the room for a rag. By the time she found one, Beni had stuck his hands in the goop and smeared it all over.

As she wiped him down, she considered the schoolroom, but only for half a second. The Turtle's room was nearby. The great hall had plenty of space and was deserted at night, but the noise of the blades would carry too far, and the wall of windows opened onto the loggia where the watchman would pass. She was running out of options.

Catalina returned carrying a rag doll in a red flowered dress. She knelt beside Beni who grabbed the doll with one wet hand and shook it. Catalina tickled Beni's tummy and he grabbed her finger with his free hand, sticking it in his mouth.

Catalina glowed. "Just imagine, in a few years, our children will be playing together."

Francesca faked a smile, but her jaw and shoulder muscles tightened.

Catalina lifted Beni. She cuddled him and hummed as she rocked him, her face serene.

Francesca's eyes smarted and she blinked. Why couldn't she be like Catalina?

"I can see you with children, Catalina. You'll be a wonderful mother, but me…" Francesca couldn't contemplate her future with anything but dread.

"All you need is some practice," Catalina said.

"I don't want practice. And I don't want to have children."

Catalina hugged Beni tighter. "You don't need to be afraid, modern medicine—"

"I'm not afraid. It's not just the birth. It's all the rest."

Catalina tilted her head. "You don't want them *ever*?"

Francesca shrugged, hurt by the accusation in Catalina's voice. "I want to go places, see things. I don't know. Maybe there's something wrong with me."

"I'm sure you'll change your mind. And when you have children of your own, you'll feel differently. You might enjoy it," Catalina said. "Just think, you could read adventure stories to them every night."

Francesca hoped her smile didn't look too much like a grimace. She didn't want to read about adventures, she wanted to have them.

Beni gave a quavering whimper and his face turned red. Catalina rocked and shushed him. Then, with a big inhale he began a high-pitched wail. "Maybe he's hungry," Catalina said over the noise.

"Why don't you take him to the family dining room?" Francesca nearly shouted as Beni's screams seemed to pierce her skull. Chef Amico usually had a few snacks set out this time of day. "I'll get some milk from the kitchen and meet you there."

Francesca didn't wait for Catalina to respond before she rushed from the room. She hurried downstairs, past the pantry, and into the smell of baking bread. As she entered the bustling kitchen, Chef Amico paused, a dab of flour on his left cheek. "Mistress, I wasn't expecting you yet."

"Don't mind me," Francesca said. "I only need a little milk for the Aquino child. I'll get it myself."

She hauled open the heavy oak door that led down to the cellar and ducked inside. The door creaked closed behind her. The cool, peaceful quiet was lovely. She paused a moment to savor it and let her eyes adjust.

The cellar was dark, lit only by the golden glow of a few candles on wall sconces. The vaulted stone ceilings had been carved out of the rock that the salle stood on, though some of the farther archways were lined with stones or bricks. The right side of the main chamber held racks of foodstuffs. Curing hams hung next to shelves filled with pale wheels of cheese. Smoked fish and plucked fowl lent a pungent odor to the chill. Barrels of grains and baskets of mushrooms and dried fruits took up another wall.

Francesca hurried down the stone stairs but tripped on the second to last step. She stumbled into a barrel next to the stairs. The cask teetered off its crate and crashed to the stone floor, scattering scrap metal across the room with a horrendous clatter.

As the noise echoed through the stone chambers, Francesca cringed and waited for a reprimand or at least an inquiry from upstairs. None came.

She hauled the barrel upright and piled the scrap metal back into it—broken candlesticks, bent utensils, pot handles that had fallen off, pans and kettles with holes, and twisted bits that she couldn't identify, all destined for the tinker's hammer. She needed help, however, to set the barrel back up onto the crate.

She went back upstairs to Chef Amico. "Could someone give me a hand?"

"With the milk?" the chef asked, puzzled.

"No, the scrap barrel. I knocked it over."

Chef Amico nodded and waved to one of the servant boys turning the spit in the fireplace. "Enrico."

Enrico followed Francesca back down into the cellar and they lifted the barrel back onto the crate. "Didn't you hear the noise?" she asked. "It made a horrible racket."

Enrico shook his head of dark curly hair. "No, mistress."

Francesca thanked him. As he headed up, she looked around the cellar.

There was more than enough space, no windows to give them away, and no one would hear a thing! She hooted out loud as she lifted her arms and spun in a circle. She and Phillip could fence here and no one would ever know! Sneaking in and out might be a challenge, but the same was true no matter where they fenced.

She went through one of the archways to where barrels, casks, and bottles of wine and spirits sat, along with a barrel of fresh milk. As she ladled milk into an empty pitcher she laughed, the sound echoing merrily around the stone walls. She went upstairs with a grin.

When Francesca walked into the family dining room, she nearly dropped the pitcher. Catalina and Sebi were kissing. They sat next to each other at the table, with Beni on Catalina's lap chewing a crust of bread.

Francesca closed the door sharply and the two jumped apart.

"Are you mad?" hissed Francesca. "Papa and your parents are next door. They could have seen!" Papa's office was next to the dining room.

Sebi ran a hand through his dark, disheveled hair and Catalina shifted Beni on her lap.

"Let them," Sebi said. "I'm tired of sneaking around."

"Now I know you've gone insane," Francesca said as she moved toward them. "Remember Antonio and Viola? Catalina will be sent away."

"It's not the same," Catalina said tucking a stray hair into place. "She was a parlor maid. It's not as if Sebi and my stations are *so* different."

Francesca stopped in her tracks as Sebi took Catalina's hand. "None of us bleed blue," he said. "Antonio will inherit; I don't see what difference it makes who I choose to marry."

"But—" Francesca said.

"Think of it," Sebi said. "Catalina would be your sister."

My sister! What a wonderful thought. Seeing them with Beni, she could easily imagine what a lovely little family Catalina and Sebi would make—if allowed. Catalina's parents were well-to-do silk merchants while the DiCesares were landed farmers, except for Papa of course. And Papa had fame, wealth, and connections. Not an impossible match. Then she'd never have to worry about Catalina being sent away. *We'd always be together. Unless Papa sends me away.* She pushed down that thought.

"Do you really think they would agree?" Francesca asked.

Catalina and Sebi's eyes met and held. "It's possible," Catalina said. "If we handle this properly."

Sebi turned toward Francesca. "Not a word to anyone until we've sorted it out. Can you do that?"

Francesca nodded, grinning. She thought about the cellar. If there was one thing she was good at, it was keeping secrets.

CHAPTER 6
ENQUIRES

Francesca was in a grand mood when she, Catalina, and Beni returned to the nursery. Soon she'd be fencing with Phillip and in the future, she might have Catalina as a sister. She was so happy, she didn't even mind Beni's occasional fits, though she was relieved when he fell asleep in the crib. As noon approached, the door opened, and Signora Aquino joined them.

Elegant and graceful, Signora Aquino was everything Francesca thought a mother should be. Francesca loved Nana with all her heart, but she'd been a tiny, lean woman, bent with age, who had a practical nature and a wicked sense of humor. Signora Aquino was grace itself. Her coiffed raven hair framed a perfect face. She wore a beautiful wine-colored silk brocade dress with cream petticoats and matching ruffles at the neckline and cuffs—no doubt one of the benefits of being wife to a silk merchant.

Francesca rose, elated. She and Catalina went to her. Signora Aquino took their hands.

"Welcome, signora," Francesca said. "I'm so glad you've come!"

"Thank you, Francesca. It's so lovely to see you again. Your father tells me how much you and Catalina are enjoying your time together."

Francesca felt a rush of warmth toward Catalina's mother. Perhaps she would be sympathetic to Catalina and Sebi.

"Catalina is like a sister to me," Francesca said glancing at Catalina. "I don't know what I would do without her."

"Treasure these days," she replied. "They can be so fleeting."

Francesca's stomach tightened. *Fleeting? What did she mean by that?* She cast a worried glance at Catalina who looked worried as well.

Signora Bianchi appeared, looking even more angular and clumsy in comparison with Signora Aquino's softly rounded figure and flowing movements.

"Lunch will be served shortly on the lawn in front of the formal gardens," the governess said. "I'll see to the little one."

"Thank you, signora," Signora Aquino said.

Catalina put one arm around her mother's waist and the other around Francesca as they headed toward the stairs. Francesca hugged Catalina for including her in the reunion with her mother.

"How are your lessons progressing, girls?" asked Signora Aquino, her voice soft and rich.

Francesca glanced over at her governess who carried Beni. She imagined the same question coming from Signora Bianchi in her harsh, matter-of-fact voice. One made her want to shine, the other made her want to cringe.

"Catalina is wonderful at sums," Francesca said. "She can do them in her head faster than Signor Gallo."

Catalina blushed. "Francesca speaks three languages," she told her mother. "Four if you count the Spanish she learned from her previous governess." Catalina turned to Francesca, teasing. "It would be five if you'd do your Latin lessons."

Signora Aquino laughed. "You two are so accomplished! I'm so very proud of both of you."

Francesca basked in the compliment. She got little praise from the signora.

The entry hall was full of the hubbub and clatter of students finding seats for lunch in the great hall beyond. Francesca glanced in, hoping to get a glimpse of Phillip, but he was nowhere to be seen. She wanted to rush in and tell him about the cellar, but it would have to wait until their Italian tutoring session this evening. If all went well, perhaps she would get to fence tonight!

Near the far stairs, Signor Aquino stood chatting with Enzo and a Spanish student, Leandro. Catalina's father, a big man who hunched a bit, perhaps to hide his height, was shaking hands with Leandro.

Leandro sported black curls, a neatly trimmed goatee, and coal-black eyes. *His sense of distance is perfect and his point control excellent,* mused Francesca as she, Catalina, and Signora Aquino approached. The gentlemen bowed to them.

"What about you, Leandro?" Catalina's father said, continuing the conversation they had interrupted. "Will you be joining your parents soon?"

Leandro's father was vice governor of Cartagena, in the New World.

"When I've learned all I can here, I may join them. Or Father may wish for me to take over the business in Spain."

"Have you been to the Americas?" Francesca asked Leandro. She could think of few things more exciting. She'd nearly memorized William Dampier's travel log about the hidden tribes of Indians, dense jungles, flesh-eating fish, and strange sea cows, not to mention snakes large enough to swallow a man whole. How amazing it would be to see such things!

"I have. Cartagena is terribly provincial," Leandro said. "They lack many of the finer things, but the climate is superb and nearly anything will grow there."

Finer things? Who needs finer things when they have fascinating ones? Francesca thought, disappointed with Leandro's lack of imagination.

"What about the natives?" she asked.

Leandro waved a hand. "The savages have been tamed or killed. It's not as wild as it once was."

Catalina's parents nodded and smiled, but his words made Francesca sad. Perhaps that was the way of progress, but wild seemed so much more interesting.

When Papa, Antonio, and Sebastian joined them, Leandro took that as his cue to bow to the Aquinos, wish them a pleasant visit, and join the other students.

The two families were loud and animated at lunch around a long table under the ancient oak that stood beside the gardens.

As Francesca watched Catalina and her mother talk together, her heart ached, not only for Nana, but for the mother she never knew.

When Francesca was eight, she had helped Nana gather roses for the floral displays. Francesca carried the basket and knife, and Nana, leaning on her cane, pointed out which flowers she wanted Francesca to collect.

"Your mother designed this garden to be just like the one at her home in England," Nana said.

"I never knew that." Francesca looked around with fresh eyes. Roses from deepest red, to brightest yellow, to purest white perfumed the air. Their colors blended and contrasted in delightful ways. She felt closer to her mother knowing she was walking through something her mother had created.

"What was she like, Nana?"

Nana limped to a nearby bench and sank down, rubbing her bad leg. "Such spirit. Just like you, dear." She patted the bench to invite Francesca to sit beside her. "She always had some new plan or idea that seemed impossible, until she did it." She gestured to the garden around them. "Like this. She had these roses brought all the way from England and planted them herself."

Francesca inhaled the sweet scent and fought back tears. "She must have been wonderful. Until I…"

"Until you what, dear?"

"Until I killed her."

Nana's eyes widened. "Who put such an idea into your head?"

Francesca leaned into her nana's soft shoulder. "Well, she died on my birthday. Papa always seems angry if I ask about it. I thought—"

"No, no, Francesca." Nana took her hand. "He's not angry at you. You are not to blame."

"Then what happened?"

Nana gave Francesca an appraising look, then shook her head and looked off into the distance. "Your parents had come to Solerno to take care of me after the fall that broke my hip. Barbary corsairs, slavers, came raiding along the coast."

Francesca gave a small gasp. She'd heard tales of the Barbary pirates' ruthlessness.

Nana's grip on her hand tightened until it hurt. "They attacked the town. Your parents and I took ship, trying to outrun them. But one of their ships was too quick." Nana's eyes glistened with tears. "We couldn't escape. We knew we'd have to fight or be sold into slavery. Imagine! Most of us were merchants and their families, or sailors, except for your father, of course."

Francesca sat up straight. "Did my mother help fight?"

Nana puckered her brow. "She was prepared to. Despite being large with you, she stood guard in the hall outside the cabin where I and the other women and children hid. That's the kind of woman she was, fearless."

Francesca swelled with pride. She imagined her mother ready to face down the pirates.

Nana shook her head. "She never got the chance. Oh, my dear, it was horrible, cannonballs flying everywhere.

Nana put a hand to her neck and focused on Francesca. "A cannonball came though the ship, and she was hit in the neck with a large splinter of wood. The doctor couldn't stop the bleeding. We would have lost you too if the doctor hadn't taken you from your mother's belly." Nana caressed Francesca's cheek. "Her last words were 'Save Francesco.'" She gave a small smile. "We thought you were going to be a boy."

"Pirates killed her," said Francesca, mostly to herself. *I was in a pirate battle!* Emotions roiled through her. "How come Papa never told me?"

Nana sighed. "It's too painful. When she died, he, well, he snapped." She looked away. "He saved us. Your father's sword arm saved us all. But it was dreadful. Afterwards he blamed himself for her death. If he hadn't taught her to fence, she would have been with the rest of the women. She would have been safe."

Nana rose to her feet and Francesca followed her on through the garden. "I never saw a man who loved a woman as much as your father loved your mother. Even after all this time, he's still heartbroken."

Francesca looked across the lunch table as Papa talked with Signor Aquino. She couldn't imagine him fighting pirates. But over the years she'd come to recognize his heartache in the way his eyes lingered on the portrait of her mother in the dining room each morning.

One day she'd found him sitting by himself, staring at the painting. When she asked him about her, he said that the things he remembered most were how smart she was, how often she laughed, and how much she loved to dance. Francesca couldn't help but wonder why he had hired a governess who discouraged all those things.

Francesca tilted her face up, watched the leaves flutter across the bright sun, and let the memories go. Nana used to say that if one focused on the past, one missed the beauty of the present and the possibility of the future. Francesca closed her eyes, content to listen to the clatter of silverware and the easy flow of conversation and laughter around the table. How wonderful it would be when they were all one family.

Papa cleared his throat. "Sebastian, Antonio, I'll see to our guests. I believe you have lessons to attend."

"Yes, sir," they said, rising and taking their leave, though Sebi's eyes were on Catalina.

When they had left, Catalina's father put a hand on Enzo's shoulder.

"Francesca—" Papa said, but Catalina's father cut in.

"She might as well hear this too. It involves Catalina, and you know how girls will talk anyway."

Francesca's stomach knotted and she saw Catalina's breath quicken. Catalina's mother took her daughter's hand.

"Catalina," Signor Aquino continued. "Enzo will be leaving the salle next week."

"So soon?" Catalina said in surprise.

"Indeed," said her father. "I hadn't intended for this all to happen so quickly, but events have been fortuitous. As the Maestro is leaving to go abroad, he has kindly agreed to take Enzo with him as his assistant as far as England."

Next week! Francesca thought.

"England!" Catalina said. "But why?"

Signor Aquino rubbed his chin. "I don't wish to get into a discussion of economics. Silk production is up in England, France has banned importation, markets have dried up. Suffice it to say, our business situation has become difficult. As Enzo is familiar with our products and methods, we need him to find new markets for our silks."

"What are you saying?" Worry clouded Catalina's face.

Her mother put an arm around her. "We may need to sell the estate."

Catalina gasped.

The signora's words came back to Francesca, *cherish your time together, it can be so fleeting.* A lump of ice lodged in her belly. Catalina's service as Francesca's companion paid for Enzo's tuition. If Enzo was no longer a student ...

Francesca took Catalina's free hand. "You can't take Catalina away!"

Catalina looked at her, frightened and confused. Francesca squeezed her hand tighter.

"She will remain here for the time being," said Signor Aquino. He turned to Catalina, "The Maestro has kindly agreed to forward your wages directly to me."

The frozen chunk in Francesca's stomach thawed a little.

He continued. "But you should know that the timetable has been accelerated. I had hoped Catalina could spend another year with you, Francesca, but I've made inquiries into a match for Catalina that will benefit our whole family. I don't wish to say more until I've received a reply."

Francesca's eyes flew to Catalina, and she bit her lip to keep from blurting out Sebi's name. She'd promised she wouldn't say anything, but why not Sebi? Her family may not have any direct connections to the silk trade, but they could help, somehow, couldn't they?

Catalina stared into the distance, her cheeks pale, her eyes unfocused. She looked too overwhelmed to say anything.

"Now, I have letters of introduction to write and much to attend to." He turned to Catalina's mother. "My dear, if you would see to the little one, I'll be along shortly."

Francesca hovered in the background as Catalina and Enzo said farewell to their parents. Just before she left, Signora Aquino took Catalina's face in her hands and spoke very softly to her. She leaned her forehead against Catalina's for a moment, kissed her on the cheek, and then climbed into the carriage.

They waved goodbye as the carriage clattered out of the gate. Francesca and Catalina retreated to Francesca's bedroom.

Catalina sat on the bed staring at her hands in her lap. "I can't believe there's no more money."

Francesca moved to the bed next to Catalina. "They can't mean *no* money."

Wealth was something Francesca had never given much thought. Some of the servants had little enough, but they never wanted for comfort. They worked hard and they were cared for. But she had seen people with no money in Cascina begging in the streets for a mouthful of food or a warm place to sleep.

She would never let that happen to Catalina, but what about her parents? There was little she could do to help. *Perhaps I can convince the head housekeeper to buy new silk drapes for the great hall and the family dining room. It's not much, but it's something.*

Francesca put an arm around Catalina. "You'll always have a home here." She thought for a moment. "Perhaps this isn't all bad. Perhaps your parents will be more receptive to a marriage between you and Sebi. Why didn't you say something?"

Catalina wiped her eyes. "You heard Father, he's already made inquiries. I don't see how Sebi can help my family, and what if we have to spend my dowry? What if your father doesn't think I'm a good match?"

Francesca wrapped her arms around Catalina. "There's still time. Everything will be all right. Enzo's smart and people like him. He'll have business back to normal in no time." She tried to sound more certain than she felt.

Catalina gave her a weak smile.

"Sebi won't care about the dowry, and Papa won't either. I'm sure of it." Francesca hoped she was right. She knew Papa wouldn't care about the money, but a dowry was also about status and reputation. He might feel it was a matter of honor.

"Do you have any idea to whom they may have made inquiries?" asked Francesca, suppressing a shiver.

Catalina wiped her eyes and shook her head. "No, but..." her voice caught, and tears came.

"What is it?" asked Francesca.

Catalina took a breath. "Mother said to remember that it doesn't matter who I marry. Any husband can give a woman good children. That's a woman's compensation." Catalina buried her face in Francesca's shoulder and cried.

Francesca smoothed Catalina's hair and did her best to comfort her, but anger burned inside her. How dare Catalina's father fail at business and then sell off his daughter to fix his own shortcomings! He couldn't treat Catalina like a pawn to be moved around the board at his pleasure.

Catalina loved Sebi and Sebi loved her. They should be together.

They would be. Francesca would not allow Catalina's father's failure to doom her to a horrible life just because she'd been born female.

CHAPTER 7
THE MAESTRO

Francesca left Catalina's room emotionally exhausted. Catalina had gone to find Sebi and break the horrible news, so Francesca made her way up to the schoolroom where Phillip and Signor Gallo were already working on Phillip's Italian.

She stopped in the doorway. Phillip sat hunched over one of the twenty desks with his arms propped on his elbows and his hands gripping handfuls of his gold hair.

The Turtle stood over him, hands behind his back, which emphasized his wide expanse of stomach covered in a lemon-colored waistcoat. The yellow belly, bald head, and dark, round-rimmed glasses made his resemblance to a turtle impossible to miss.

"*Di fare la sua conoscenza, signore,*" Signor Gallo was saying.

"What does *conoscenza* mean again?" Phillip asked.

The Turtle waved a hand impatiently. "Eets, ah…" He searched for the English word.

"Acquaintance," Francesca said from the doorway. "He's saying he's pleased to meet you. As am I, Lord Worthington."

She came forward as the signore nodded. "*Grazie, signorina.* Dat ees it."

Phillip shot her a grateful look as he rose, bowed, and said hello. He turned to the headmaster. "Thank you, signore, but I fail to see how 'It's a pleasure to meet you' is helpful since I've already met most everyone here."

"Basics, basics," The Turtle said. "You must start at da beginning. Is dat not so, little mistress."

Francesca gave him a smile.

"In the meantime, I'm falling behind in all my classes," Phillip said.

Signor Gallo waved a hand as if shooing away Phillip's concerns. "Dat cannot be helped." He turned to Francesca, leaning forward so she got a strong dose of his breath. "What can I do for you, mistress?"

She leaned slightly away. She'd prepared her excuse ahead of time. "I had a small question about today's Latin lesson, but I can see you both have larger concerns."

Signor Gallo and Phillip both nodded.

"I'll say," Phillip said. "Like, how am I supposed to do my schoolwork?"

Signor Gallo shook his head. "You cannot run before you can walk, and I cannot spend all day teaching you. I have too many works to do."

"Perhaps I could be of assistance," Francesca said.

"You, signorina?" The Turtle stretched his neck forward then drew it back again like his namesake.

"You need to work with Lord Worthington on the basics, but he also needs someone to help him translate his lessons into English and his schoolwork into Italian. I suppose I could help with the second part, for a little while."

"No, no, no," said The Turtle, wagging a finger. "You will fall behind in your own lessons."

Francesca nodded thoughtfully. "I'm sure you're right, as always, signore." She turned to go. "And I know you won't mind doing all the extra work yourself."

She took two steps.

"*Un momento,* signorina."

She turned back to see Phillip hiding a smile from The Turtle. She kept her face polite but neutral.

"On a second of a thought, your lessons are not so different."

"I have felt that my English is not as good as it once was," added Francesca. "It would be a good opportunity to work on it."

"I'd be happy to help with that," Phillip said.

"Si, it could be arranged."

"Perhaps if we met here in the evenings," Phillip said.

"Under your watchful eye, of course," Francesca added. "While you work on the next day's lessons."

"Si, si, I will speak with the signora." He turned to walk back to his desk at the front of the room waving a hand. "Tomorrow."

While his back was turned Francesca leaned down and whispered in Phillip's ear, "Meet me in the kitchen at midnight. I'll bring the blades."

Just after midnight, the golden light of Francesca's candle sent shadows swaying and lurching around the vaulted stone arches as she descended the steps into the cellar. The pungent smells of cheese and aging meats filled her nose. She shivered at the chill and at the delicious anticipation that coursed through her. She felt a twinge of guilt that she was so happy when Catalina was facing such an uncertain and frightening future, but there was nothing she could do for Catalina at the moment.

At the top of the stairs, Phillip swung the oak-slab door shut. The breeze made the glow from Francesca's candle dance, sending shadows reeling around them. Phillip held her old practice blade—which she had straightened and shined as best she could—as well as a newer practice foil that glinted in the light. He hesitated at the top of the stairs.

"Are you sure about this?" His voice echoed around the stone chambers. He ran a hand through his hair. "I know I promised, but this seems … dangerous."

Her stomach tightened. He couldn't back out now. "No one will hear a thing. I checked," Francesca said, trying to sound nonchalant. Secretly she agreed with him. The element of risk made it all the more exciting.

"What if someone wanders down here?" he said.

"I'll be in trouble, certainly, but I've been thinking. I can tell them that I forced you to fence with me."

Phillip gave an amused huff and twisted his mouth to one side. "And how exactly would you force me to fence with you?"

"Well, like Pietro, I threatened to tell the other students that you insulted them."

"And they'd believe that?" Phillip said with a laugh.

She tilted her head to one side. "They might."

"If they did, wouldn't that get you in even more trouble?"

Francesca shrugged. "As you say in England, 'in for a penny, in for a pound.'"

"Are you quite positive it's worth it?" Phillip finally came down the stairs to stand in front of her, his blue eyes intent on her face.

"Yes. Completely. Beyond a doubt."

She held his eyes, willing him to understand.

"I thought about how you must feel, with everyone fencing except you," he said. "It must be lonely."

She nodded as her throat tightened.

"I know something about that."

He was quiet for a moment and a shadow of pain crossed his face. Francesca wanted to ask a million questions but didn't dare. She reached out to touch his arm, but before she did, he shook his head, suddenly brisk. "If I'm to be your fencing maestro, we're going to do it right. We start with simple footwork and drilling, just like class. What the maestro says is law. No arguing."

She nodded, relieved. "Of course."

"Very well then."

Francesca shivered, partly with anticipation and partly with the bite in the air as she set the candle on a barrel in the corner. Then she moved into the open and hiked up her skirts a few inches. Phillip handed her a blade, the metal cold on her palm.

Francesca saluted Phillip, raising the tip of her practice blade toward the ceiling and then slashing it downward. Phillip returned the gesture. She dropped into *en garde* position, right shoulder forward, knees bent, back straight.

Phillip had Francesca do footwork. He stood near the stairs calling softly, "Advance, lunge, retreat, crossover, parry." Francesca obeyed as she moved back and forth across the stone floor.

It was wonderful to have space for nearly two dozen steps before she had to turn around, instead of the ten steps in her room. Soon she no longer felt the chill. She glowed with warmth and happiness.

"Halt," Phillip commanded when Francesca was stretched into a lunge. He walked around her, examining her form. "You're leaning too far forward on your lunges. You have to keep your weight better balanced so that you can retreat quickly."

Francesca opened her mouth to argue that she'd been doing this for years, but then shut it again. He was the maestro, and this was what she had asked for—what she needed. She corrected her position and tried a retreat. The move was definitely quicker. It would take a while to remember; she realized she had years of bad habits to break.

Next Francesca and Phillip practiced high-line parries, and having his blade to parry against was a joy. The shockwaves through her arm when their blades clanked together surprised her, and she found herself clutching the hilt of her blade too tightly. Sebi had been right about one thing: practicing parries without another blade had just been waving a foil around. She learned more in half an hour against a real blade than in nine years against an imagined one.

Once the candle had burned down an inch, Phillip called a halt. "That's all for tonight."

Francesca bit back her disappointment and the protest on her lips. He was right. They needed their rest. They'd have plenty more chances to practice together.

As Francesca lifted the candle from the barrel, she realized how tired her arm and hand were from the parry drills. Her muscles shook, her fingers twitched, and the candle slipped from her grasp.

The darkness was absolute.

"What happened?" Phillip said somewhere behind her.

"Nothing, nothing. I just dropped the candle." *Stupid. Stupid.* Now she looked like an idiot. And everything had been going so well. She knelt, her fingers sweeping the cold stone floor. "I'll find it. It can't have rolled far."

"Well, we were going upstairs anyway. Do we need a candle?"

"I wouldn't want Chef Amico to find it and get suspicious," Francesca said.

"Good point. I'll help you." His voice moved nearer. "Where are you?"

"I'm down here." She reached out in the direction of his voice and found nothing but air. She wondered if he was reaching for her too. Then her fingers brushed against fabric. Was that his leg, his arm? His hand closed around hers and he knelt beside her. His nearness and his touch made her pulse race. She could imagine his blue eyes searching for her.

"I'm usually not so clumsy," she said.

"Don't worry, we'll find it."

He let go. She wanted to reach for him again, but she could hear the rustle of his clothing and his hands dragging back and forth across the floor. Right. The candle.

On her knees, she swept her hands across the stone and along the base of a barrel. As she swung in an arc to her left, she cracked her temple against something solid. Yellow stars exploded in the utter blackness.

"Owww," Francesca cried.

"Uch," Phillip groaned.

One of his warm hands found her left shoulder. She turned to face him.

"You have a hard head," he said.

"You're not the first person to say so," Francesca replied. "Though usually they don't mean it so literally."

Phillip laughed, his hand leaving a patch of heat on her shoulder. The warmth rippled through her. Kneeling upright, Francesca reached forward, and her hand found his chest, his heart beating against her palm.

"That was your head too?" she asked, a little breathlessly. She cleared her throat.

"My cheekbone."

The fingers of her other hand slid up his shoulder and neck until they brushed his cheek, invisible in the darkness. "Sorry," she said, a little awed at her own boldness. His heart seemed to beat faster beneath her other palm, or did she imagine it?

He moved closer and she could sense the heat of his body in front of her. He smelled faintly of worn leather and green pastures.

"What's another bruise more or less," he said.

Francesca licked her lips. He was so close, all she had to do was lean forward and she'd be against him. She discovered she was shaking. The cellar was so cold. How warm he would feel. She could wrap her arms around him—

"I, well, uh," he said. "How did I do? I mean, as your maestro?"

"Perfect," she said, but she was thinking about how close they were. She'd never kissed a boy before. How would it feel?

"Do you, are you ... less lonely?" He said the last part in a whisper that felt achingly intimate in the darkness.

Warmth tingled in her cheeks and spread downward. What was it about him that made her want things she'd never wanted before? "Much," she whispered back, leaning still closer. She felt his warm breath on her face. She imagined their lips meeting, but instead, he moved away, and her palm that had been against his chest suddenly felt empty and chilled. Disappointment washed through her, draining the heat.

"Back home," he said. "My father ... well, I was lonely there too."

His father, the nobleman.

Loss curled through her. He was the eldest son of a lord. Of course he had been lonely with only servants and underlings like her around. He might not be as snobbish and superior as the other nobles at the salle, but he was one of them all the same. He couldn't possibly be having the same thoughts she was. She'd look like a fool if ...

She sat back on her heels.

"You're not alone here," she said. "There are plenty of other noblemen."

Phillip was quiet for a dozen heartbeats.

"Perhaps we should go up and get another candle," he said.

"I guess we should."

Once they'd found the stairs and inched their way up, the kitchen seemed bright in comparison. They found a spare candle in the pantry, lit it from the embers banked down in the cookfire, and headed back down.

Phillip relit the first candle. After they hid the foils in a back corner of the cellar under some old tarps, Phillip suggested she go up first.

She took one of the candles and paused at the cellar door to look back at Phillip, golden in the candlelight. "Thank you, maestro. I already can't wait until tomorrow night."

He smiled. "Me too."

As Francesca made her way through the silent kitchen and great hall and up the stairs, she tried to analyze all the new feelings and desires that had swirled through her in the dark. They frightened her a little, but she liked that.

She wondered if that was the way Catalina felt with Sebi. If so, they *had* to be allowed to marry. It wouldn't be fair to take that from her and force her to marry someone she didn't care for. Francesca wanted to talk to Catalina about her feelings for Phillip, but she didn't dare. If she revealed her late-night fencing class, Catalina and Sebi might try to stop her.

Still, for the first time, she could imagine why other girls wanted to marry. Could those feelings be enough? Could they make up for a lifetime of dull duty and responsibility? Could love be enough of an adventure? She wished she knew.

CHAPTER 8
COMPETITIONS

A week later, Francesca said goodbye to Papa in his office, where he straightened the last few papers on his desk. He wore a tan riding jacket with a light travel cloak to keep off the road dust. She missed him already. He gave her a hug and kissed each cheek. "I expect you to obey Signora Bianchi while I'm away," he told her, hands on her shoulders and looking sternly into her eyes. "I know she's strict, but she only—"

"Wants what's best for me," Francesca finished for him. "I'll do my best, Papa."

He smiled and brushed the tip of her nose with his finger. "And we both know how good that will be."

Francesca smiled and he held her tight. She breathed in his fresh, spicy scent—the smell that made her feel safe and loved. She fixed it in her mind to sustain her until he returned.

"I was a lot like you when I was young," he said. "Whatever I was told *not* to do was suddenly the most interesting thing in the world." He pulled on a pair of kid gloves. "Sometimes I wish there were a little less of me and more of your mother in you. She, well, she found joy everywhere."

Francesca treasured every scrap Papa let fall about her mother, despite the sadness they engendered.

"I love you, Papa. I wish you weren't going."

"We must all do our duty. I'll return as soon as I'm able."

Or better yet, she wished she were going with him. How exciting it would be to watch the bullfights of Madrid, see the throngs of people along the Grand Promenade of Paris, and meet some of Europe's greatest fencers. But that would never happen, and with Catalina about to be married off … a mantle of gray settled over her.

Together they walked down the stairs and out into the courtyard where all the students had gathered. The young men snapped to attention with blades in hand—except for Sebastian, Antonio, and Enzo, who waited near the gate and held the reins of four horses. The servants too had come to see Papa off and stood behind the students with their hands clasped. Catalina, beside Enzo, slid one arm through his. Outside the gate a dapple had been harnessed to a laden cart.

At a sign from Antonio, the pupils brought their blades vertical, then slashed them toward the ground in a salute to Papa.

"Gentlemen," Papa said. "I leave you in the capable hands of Maestro Ferro. Antonio will instruct the first-year students. They both have much to teach you. I expect to see improvement in all your skills when I return."

Maestro Ferro, who'd stepped in for Papa before, had newly come from Florence. He shook Papa's hand. He was a few inches taller than Papa, slender, with thinning brown hair and goatee, but lacking Papa's imposing presence. *Not nearly as good as Papa with backsword or rapier, but his cape work is better*, thought Francesca.

Papa mounted his horse and turned to the students. "I expect you all to act honorably while I'm away. What is the code we live by?"

The students replied in unison. "To defend God and country. To keep one's word. To defend the weak and innocent. To never abandon a noble cause. To avoid lying and cheating. To exhibit courage in word and deed."

Francesca stared with jealousy at Antonio and Sebastian as the others continued. Her brothers were riding as far as Cascina with Papa, but because of Signora Bianchi's insistence, Francesca would remain home.

"To live for freedom, justice, and all that is good. To die with honor," the students recited.

"Well done," Papa said. "These laws protect us from our baser natures and serve as a path to righteousness and contentment. Follow the path and you'll live with a clear conscience and light heart. Adieu."

Catalina and Enzo said their goodbyes, then Papa turned his bay horse and the travelers started out of the courtyard. Francesca leaned against the wrought-iron gate as they cantered down the hill.

"I wish they weren't leaving," Catalina said as she wiped away tears.

"I suppose you'll be leaving me soon, too," Francesca said glumly.

Catalina took her arm to head back toward the salle before the signora came looking for them.

"We'll always be friends," Catalina said. "No matter where we are."

"Sisters would be so much better. When are you going to talk to your parents about Sebi?"

Catalina shrugged. "Sebi's going to speak with your father on the ride. If your father agrees, it'll be up to him to contact my parents."

"There must be something more we can do."

"It's out of our hands."

"I hate that," muttered Francesca.

Catalina squeezed her arm. "I know you do. You always want to fix things, but our duty is to obey our parents. I must think about my family, not just myself."

They passed through the main doors into the entry.

"But the other day—"

"I was caught off guard and upset." Catalina stopped and faced Francesca. "After all my parents have given me, I'm glad I can do something for them."

Hurt and betrayal lodged in Francesca's chest. "But, you love Sebi!" she said, trying to keep her voice low. "At least you said you did." Her words came out more accusatory than she'd intended.

"Of course I do!"

"Then how can you give up so easily? How can you let your father do this to you?"

Francesca spotted Signora Bianchi descending the stairs toward them.

"Do you think this is easy?" Catalina raised her voice. "Do you think this is what I want? Not all of us can afford to be selfish."

Francesca bristled. "It's not about being selfish, it's about being honest!"

"And what would you know about that!" snapped Catalina. She glanced toward their governess and dropped her voice. "We're always having to come up with excuses for you. Have you heard nothing your father says about honor?"

Francesca turned away from Catalina, stung.

Signora Bianchi paused on the stairs. "Girls! Lower your voices! It's unladylike."

"Yes, signora," Catalina said.

"Francesca, Signora Moreno is waiting for you. That wool is not going to card and spin itself, and the chef is expecting you when you finish." The signora tucked an escaped hair back into her sever bun. "Catalina, I believe Signor Gallo would like a word with you about your Latin lessons."

As Catalina climbed the stairs, Francesca glared at her back a moment, then softened.

"Francesca! You mustn't keep Signora Moreno waiting," said her governess.

"Yes, signora," she mumbled as she headed down the hall.

She hated fighting with Catalina. It made her feel small and lonely.

She realized that Catalina's words stung because they were true. She was dishonest, pretending to be someone she wasn't, but what other option did she have? The world wouldn't accept her. Could she suppress her true self to be who the world wanted her to be, like Catalina was doing? She didn't think she was strong enough. Catalina was so selfless to sacrifice her own happiness for her family, but there had to be some way she wouldn't have to.

She paused out of eyesight of her governess and turned toward the library. There she scanned the floor-to-ceiling shelves. She knew little about the silk trade, other than that silk was made by the silkworm. If she was going to help Catalina, she needed to know more. Her search netted two volumes, one on the cultivation of the worms and weaving of the fabric, and one on the history of the silk trade. She snuck them to her room before hurrying to the sewing room.

———⌐———

At midnight a few days later, Francesca waited impatiently in the cellar for Phillip to arrive.

That morning she'd snuck from the spinning wheel to the window while Signora Morello was in the next room. The signora was yelling at the maid Maria for tearing a sheet as she changed Signor Gallo's linens. Francesca figured the signora would be at it for a while.

Luckily, the sewing room window overlooked the courtyard where Phillip sparred with Leandro.

Leandro fenced in the Italian style that Papa taught. His blade tip never wavered from pointing at Phillip's chest and he kept his movements tight, retreating often to wait for an opening in Phillip's defenses, patient and cat-like.

Phillip, by contrast, fenced in the English style. Francesca had read about it but never studied it in action. The English style was more active and physical; instead of waiting for openings, Phillip created them by pressing or beating Leandro's blade out of the way and then striking. He attacked quickly and often, like a terrier after a rat.

She'd been interested in which style would prevail, but beyond that, she enjoyed watching Phillip fence. Though his actions were fast and powerful, there was a grace to them that reminded Francesca of dancing.

Now, as she paced the cellar, she felt herself blush when she imagined being his partner in this intricate and dangerous dance, but so far, he'd only let her do drills.

Her heart gave an extra beat when he finally appeared at the top of the stairs. He carried two candles. With Francesca's candle, that made three. Francesca hadn't planned or even dared hope for another encounter in the dark, but it stung a little that he was working so hard to prevent one.

"Have you heard the news?" he asked.

Francesca nodded. "Your first official bout."

She'd caught the announcement at the tail end of class. Phillip would need to win at least three of his five bouts to remain at the salle. She knew he was eager to prove himself. She wished she could compete, but if she couldn't, Phillip would be her proxy. She'd help him win.

"And against Pietro. Oh, how I'd love to wipe the smug look off his face after all the grief he's given me," Phillip said, frowning.

Pietro was responsible for more than one beating that Phillip had taken at the hands of the other students.

"He's fast, but his point control is sloppy. He parries wide," Francesca told him. "Your English style is a hindrance against Pietro. There's no point beating his blade out of the way when he's doing the work for you. Your best bet is to attack outside his guard. When he parries wide, you'll have plenty of time to bring your blade around his and land your hit."

Phillip scrunched his eyebrows. Was that confusion or skepticism she read on his face?

"You're taller," she went on. "You have reach. Watch your distance. If you can stay out of his range, but in yours, you'll have an advantage."

"Look, I'm the maestro," Phillip said, "but, you're right about one thing, I do have reach on him. Some distance drills are in order tonight."

Francesca and Phillip faced each other, blades in hand, and each moved forward and backward as they changed the size of their steps and the distance between them.

There was something very intimate about being so overly conscious of the position and closeness of Phillip's body. Her heart raced.

"Halt," called Phillip.

He lunged toward Francesca, checking his distance, but the tip of his foil came up two inches short of her body. He shook his head.

Francesca tried to ignore her reeling senses and concentrate on the drill, but when she called, "Halt," and lunged toward Phillip, she was six inches off. She took a deep breath. *Get ahold of yourself. You're being ridiculous.*

They took turns calling a halt and checking distance. They nearly always came up short. Francesca was surprised. When she'd practiced in her room, she knew exactly how close she needed to be to hit her stuffed mannequin, but her mannequin stayed put. Judging distance to a live, moving object—especially one that did such strange things to her pulse—was something else entirely. She hadn't realized how complicated it could be.

When she finally succeeded and landed her point perfectly on his chest, she beamed with pride and had to resist the urge to hug him.

After an hour's practice they both had a good feel for exactly how close they needed to be to their target to land a hit.

"That's all for tonight," he said. "Let's get some rest."

Francesca nodded. She felt exhausted, as much from controlling her runaway thoughts and emotions as from the drill. Had he felt any of what she had during the drill? If so, he hid it well. "Thank you, Phillip. Good luck tomorrow," Francesca said wishing she knew what more to say. "I know you'll win."

The following morning Francesca rubbed her tired eyes. She'd been unable to sleep after the distance drill with Phillip, so she stayed up most of the night finishing the books on silk. But while interesting, they had not helped her come up with a plan to help Catalina's family—other than ordering more silk for the salle.

As fencing class started, Francesca, Catalina, and the signora worked in the sewing room. The girls had patched up their quarrel, reserving energy for their common enemy, Signora Bianchi.

Francesca sat in the sewing-room window seat repairing a hem on a tablecloth under the signora's watchful eye.

The clank and scrape of fencing foils and encouraging calls of the students wafted in through the open window. Francesca watched Phillip and Pietro moving forward and back, circling each other, waiting for openings. Francesca wished she was down there cheering Phillip on. She'd heard Sebi say that the servants were laying two-to-one odds in Pietro's favor.

Now, thought Francesca, and Phillip lunged. Pietro parried wide and Phillip landed the tip of his foil on Pietro's chest. Most of the spectators cheered.

"Francesca!"

She jumped.

"You're supposed to be repairing that tablecloth, not pulling it to pieces," the signora said.

She realized she held a section of cream linen twisted and taut between her hands. "Sorry, signora."

"Come away from that window, or we'll need a whole new tablecloth." The signora glanced out the window, twisted her mouth to one side, and set down her embroidery.

"Francesca, I know you've been tutoring Lord Worthington. I've allowed it," continued Signora Bianchi, "because Signor Gallo has been chaperoning, and because he says you've been very helpful, but you mustn't get too involved. Lord Worthington is nobility. He's a pleasant young man, but you mustn't take his friendliness as license to hope for more."

That moment in the darkness with Phillip came back to Francesca in a flash and sent warmth into her cheeks. "I know, signora." She wanted to ask how to stop herself from hoping, but that would mean admitting that she had hoped in the first place.

The signora stood. "What happens in the yard is none of your concern. Catalina, would you please switch seats with Francesca."

"Yes, signora," Catalina said, rising.

Signora Bianchi closed the window and Francesca grumbled as she plopped into the overstuffed armchair with its back to the window. It was agony to hear the cheers filtering in from the courtyard and not be able to watch. She listened for names, scores—anything to figure out what was going on, but she couldn't tell.

That night Francesca reached the cellar early and waited impatiently for Phillip.

"Well, what happened?" she asked when he finally opened the cellar door.

Phillip grinned as he bounded down the stairs. "I trounced him."

"Wonderful!" Francesca said, thrilled that Phillip was that much closer to being allowed to remain at the salle.

"It felt good to wipe that smug smile from his face. It was easy," Phillip said, "largely because of our practice last night. Acting as your maestro has made me a better fencer."

"It's helped me too."

"Yes. Your parries are much better, and—"

"No, not just my fencing." Francesca looked away, feeling self-conscious. "I'm just, happier. All my chores seem easier when I know I'll get to fence soon. I almost feel like I'm a part of the school."

Phillip moved closer to her and took his foil from her hand. "I know what you mean. It felt good to have people cheer for me today. I finally felt like I fit in."

Their eyes met. She wanted to step toward him and slide her arms around his neck, press herself against the warmth of his body, but Signora Bianchi's words echoed through her mind. *You mustn't hope for more.*

She turned away. "I'm glad."

He rested his warm hand on her arm just above the elbow. She turned back to him, and their eyes connected again.

"I have you to thank for that," he said.

Confusion filled her. Did he mean because he understood more Italian after her lessons? Or was he talking about his improved fencing skills? Or could he mean their time together? A blush spread from her face down her neck.

Please don't let him notice.

She stepped away, putting a little distance between them, and looked down at the foil in her hand. "I, well, does that mean you'll finally bout with me instead of making me do footwork and drills?"

"Whoa, there," he said. "I worked with my maestro for six months before he let me bout. First you need to master all the basics and work on your control."

"Please," Francesca said. "Just one short bout. Just a couple touches."

Phillip shook his head. "You're not ready. Besides, I've had my share of bouting for today, and I have another match tomorrow." He paused, "Against Burckhardt."

"Burckhardt! But he's been fencing much longer than you have."

"It doesn't matter. I can't wait to take that bullying ape apart."

Francesca frowned. Burckhardt won often, despite the fact that he wasn't a great fencer.

"Burckhardt's slow," Phillip said. "I can take him."

"He likes to intimidate people," Francesca said. "He'll come at you straight away. When he does—"

"I know what I'm doing."

"But, when he—"

"Thanks, I can take care of it."

"But Phillip—"

"I'm the maestro. I can win this one on my own. I need to win this one on my own."

Francesca clenched her teeth. The rebuff stung. It was so glaringly obvious to her how to defeat Burckhardt. Did he see it too?

Phillip shook his head. "You were right, by the way, about Pietro's point control. How do you know all this?"

"Because I watch," Francesca said, unable to keep the years of frustration out of her voice. "I watch and watch, because that's all I've ever been allowed to do."

"Well, you're not watching now, you're doing more footwork," Phillip said with a wry smile.

"Yes, maestro," she replied with an over-exaggerated sigh.

Phillip laughed.

When Francesca woke the next morning, a hard, steady rain turned the world outside her window gray. She smiled. That meant class, as well as Phillip's bout, would be held in the great hall instead of the courtyard. There was at least a chance she'd be able to watch—if she were clever.

She dressed, snuck to the sewing room, gathered up her embroidery in its circular frame, a few spare needles, and thread, and hurried back to her room.

Francesca was quickly fill-stitching an emerald leaf on the stomacher she was embroidering when Catalina knocked softly and entered.

"Now I've seen everything." Catalina put a hand to Francesca's forehead to mock checking her temperature. "You must be quite ill."

"Just a momentary fit of insanity," Francesca said, setting the embroidery aside. "Let's get some breakfast. Then we can talk to Signora Moreno about new silk drapes for the great hall."

Catalina gave her a hug. "I know what you're trying to do, and thank you, but it's a temporary measure at best."

"Well, temporary measures are better than none. And if I must perform all the horrid duties of the lady of the house, I ought to get my way once in a while."

Catalina chuckled. "I won't argue with that."

"Well, where is it?" asked Signora Bianchi when Francesca admitted that her embroidery was not in the sewing room.

"The rain woke me early," explained Francesca. "I couldn't sleep, so I came and got it to help me relax. It's in my room."

The signora squinted in suspicion and Catalina's face showed amusement. Finally, the signora said, "Go on then. Go get it."

Francesca hurried from the sewing room, through the sitting room and out into the hallway. Instead of heading to her room, she ducked down a flight and onto the balcony that overlooked the great hall.

The great hall's tables had been pushed aside and the benches piled in the corners, leaving the marble floor open for fencing class.

During balls, the balcony where Francesca stood held a group of musicians. She leaned over the intricate wrought-iron rail, watching the action below.

Her timing couldn't have been better. Phillip and Burckhardt were moving to the center of the floor. The difference between them was striking. Burckhardt's ash blonde hair looked dull next to Phillip's lustrous golden locks, and Phillip appeared lithe and elegant compared to Burckhardt's menacing bulk. When Phillip caught her eye and flashed her a brief, confident smile, her heart sang.

Maestro Ferro stood to one side directing the bout and Antonio stood across from him as judge to make sure the fight was fair, and no rules were broken. The rest of the class gathered in a loose circle around them. A few of the kitchen staff had stepped out of the kitchen to watch.

Burckhardt bowed stiffly when he noticed Francesca watching from the balcony, making all eyes turn to her. Her cheeks washed with heat. *Damn him. I was trying to be invisible.*

Phillip and Burckhardt saluted each other, Signor Ferro, Antonio, and then the spectators. Burckhardt made a show of saluting Francesca especially, making her cringe again.

She hoped Phillip would beat him.

Odds were not in his favor, however. Burckhardt was at least a foot taller. That gave him much greater reach. Phillip would need to get in close—inside Burckhardt's guard—in order to get him off balance. Burckhardt also had more experience than Phillip. And then there was his size. Burckhardt's presence was intimidating.

Francesca put her hand to her mouth and watched with apprehension.

Once they had taken their *en garde* positions, Signor Ferro called, "*Allay!*"

Predictably, Burckhardt attacked immediately, throwing himself toward Phillip, swinging his blade wide. *Down!* Thought Francesca, *passado sotto!* If Phillip dropped low and held out his blade, Burckhardt would run right onto it. That would give him an easy point. The strategy would only work once, but it would knock Burckhardt off balance, put him on the defensive.

Instead, Phillip backed away, parrying. Burckhardt landed a point on his chest. The students cheered.

"Halt!" called the signore.

"Point, Lord Ernst," Antonio said.

As the fencers took their *en garde* positions again, Phillip shot her a look and Francesca tried to smile back encouragement, but she knew the bout was lost. Now Phillip would be on the defensive. Burckhardt had the advantage, and he was the more experienced fencer.

The bout would go to the first fencer to land five hits on his opponent. Twice more Burckhardt came out strong, backing Phillip away and landing points.

Phillip rallied, parrying Burckhardt's next charge, and landing a blow on Burckhardt's hip. Francesca clapped and a few people cheered him on.

Burckhardt frowned when he saw Francesca cheering for Phillip and sneered as they again fell into *en garde* position. When the maestro called

"Fence!" Burckhardt attacked without his usual swinging blade. His point was steady, even, and aimed straight for Phillip's face.

Francesca gasped and clutched the rail.

Phillip jerked his head backwards, swinging his arms to keep from falling. The blade came an inch short. Burckhardt brought his blade tip down onto Phillip's chest.

"Halt!" called the signore.

Except for Phillip's and Burckhardt's heavy breathing, silence filled the room. Aiming for an opponent's face was strictly prohibited. The blades might be blunted, but they could still easily damage an eye. If he'd made a mistake, at the very least Burckhardt should offer apologies. If he did it on purpose, that was grounds for expulsion.

Anger roiled through Francesca. She knew Burckhardt's fencing well enough to know he had deliberately aimed for Phillip's face. Papa would have known too, but he wasn't here. Burckhardt had meant to hurt Phillip.

Emotions seethed across Phillip's face as the silence stretched out.

Finally, Maestro Ferro cleared his throat. "Lord Ernst—"

"My apologies, Lord Worthington," interrupted Burckhardt. "A slip, to be sure. I'll be more careful next time."

It sounded more like a threat than an apology. Francesca set her teeth.

"As will I," Phillip said, narrowing his eyes.

Signor Ferro turned to Antonio who said, "The point was good."

"Then that's enough for now. We'll conclude the bout there in Lord Ernst's favor," the maestro said.

CHAPTER 9
WHAT GOES ON HERE

Phillip's face darkened as he looked around the crowded but silent hall, though he apparently knew better than to argue with the maestro. He glanced up at Francesca, then turned away. Francesca wanted to talk to him about what had just happened, but she didn't dare in front of so many people. She would have to wait until tonight.

"Next up, Sebastian and Leandro," announced Maestro Ferro.

Francesca paused. She should head to her room to collect her embroidery and return to the signora before she was missed, but Sebi and Leandro were the two best fencers in the salle, not counting Antonio who seldom bouted. Francesca was curious to see who would win. She decided to collect her embroidery and then stop back to watch a few minutes of the match.

When she returned, the bout had already begun. She leaned on the balcony rail, watching intently.

With a feint left and a quick disengage and thrust, Sebi landed his point on Leandro's chest. The action was fast and well controlled.

"Halt!" called Maestro Ferro.

"Point, Sebastian," Antonio said.

Leandro nodded in acknowledgement.

Nicely done, but Leandro won't fall for that again, Francesca thought as she, and many of the others, cheered. Phillip cheered as well, but Burckhardt stared fixedly at her from the far side of the room. She glared at him, then turned her attention back to the fencers.

Sebi and Leandro saluted and fell into *en garde* position.

The moment that Maestro Ferro called "Fence!" both men exploded toward each other in leaping attacks called *flèches*. In midair their bodies hurtled together, blades extended. When they smashed into each other, there was a cry of pain and, a second later, the *plink* of metal against marble.

Students gasped as the action stopped. Sebi and Leandro swore. Antonio and the Maestro moved toward them.

In the press of bodies below Francesca couldn't tell what had happened.

"Christ! Pull it out!" Sebastian cried.

When Leandro stepped aside, Francesca saw that the blunted tip had broken off Leandro's practice blade. The sword stood quivered in the air, protruding from Sebastian's thigh.

Francesca watched, riveted, as Antonio supported Sebi, and the maestro plucked the sword from his leg. Sebi swore profusely as blood flowed down his thigh and calf, glaringly bright red against his white breeches and stockings.

Francesca shook herself and ran to find Signora Bianchi.

"There's been an accident," Francesca said as she burst into the sewing room, "Sebi's been hurt!"

The color drained from Catalina's face. As she rose, her embroidery fell to the floor, forgotten.

"Be specific," snapped the signora. "What's happened?"

"He's, he'll be fine, I'm sure," Francesca said quickly to reassure Catalina. "A foil broke and pierced his leg."

"Right," Signora Bianchi said. "Catalina, fetch my healer's bag. Come, Francesca."

Catalina gave a quick nod. "Yes, signora." She hurried away. Francesca and the signora headed for the main hall.

When they entered, the students were laughing, which relieved Francesca.

A bench had been carried over and Sebi lay on it, a bloodstained kerchief tied around his thigh. The other students gathered round him, and he basked in the attention.

"I should thank you, Leandro," joked Sebi. "You know how women love a battle scar."

"Do they?" Leandro grinned. "I thought they usually preferred the pin to the pincushion."

The students laughed and Francesca smiled. Sebi would milk this injury for all the sympathy and favors it was worth. The group parted to make way for Francesca and the signora.

Signora Bianchi looked down her long nose and examined the kerchief around Sebi's leg. "Who tied this?" she asked curtly.

"I did," Maestro Ferro said.

"It's too tight. Do you want him to lose the whole leg?"

"I merely wished to stop the bleeding." The maestro colored slightly.

"It must bleed a while to clean the wound." The signora untied the kerchief and Sebi muffled a groan as the blood flowed again.

Catalina appeared with the medical bag and handed it to the signora. She gave a small gasp at the blood soaked into Sebi's breeches and stockings. Sebi grinned back.

Signora Bianchi shot Catalina a look of reproach then turned to the maestro. "You needn't all stand around gawking. Sebastian will be fine, but I'd recommend he stay off the leg for a few days. We'll see to him."

"Of course, signora. I'll help in any way I can," the maestro said. He turned to the students. "Class is finished for the day. Dismissed."

As the students moved off toward the exit, Francesca noticed Catalina's hands trembling. She wondered if her own hands would be too if they were tending Phillip's wound.

"Francesca, please fetch a pair of crutches from my room," Signora Bianchi said as she pulled a fresh bandage from her bag.

"Yes, signora."

As Francesca exited the great hall, she noticed Burckhardt chatting with Leandro. She wished she had time to give Burckhardt a piece of her mind, but it would have to wait.

She went up two floors, down the hallway, through the sitting room and sewing room to Signora Bianchi's room beyond.

It was a plain chamber, severe in its lack of decoration, but at least the walls were a cheery yellow. She collected a pair of crutches from the oak armoire and hurried back.

In the sitting room, Burckhardt stood in her path with arms crossed, feet planted, and an arrogant look. He shouldn't have been there. The family's quarters were private. Students were allowed only by invitation.

Francesca stopped in her tracks, and her anger flared. He might have hurt or killed Phillip.

"You did that on purpose!" she said before she could stop herself.

"So what if I did, my lady?" He strode toward her past a pair of leather armchairs.

She clenched her hands around the crutches. "You could have put his eye out."

He waved a hand. "I only meant to scratch up that pretty face of his so you could see what he really is."

"Oh, and what is he?" She barely contained her anger.

"My family knows his of old. His father is a drunkard and a rogue."

"He is not his father."

"Really, my lady? In my experience, the apple doesn't fall far from the tree."

"So you're saying your father blinds people for no reason?" she shot back.

In two more steps he towered above her. His small gray eyes were flint-hard. He pulled the crutches from her hand and tossed them aside. "My father is not afraid to use his natural advantages, but he doesn't cheat and steal. I know you've been tutoring him. I see how you look at him. He—"

"It's none of your concern!" She sidled toward the marble fireplace, suddenly frightened by his size and closeness.

He followed. "You've seen me beat him; you know I'm the better man."

Francesca was taken aback. Burckhardt was offended that she preferred Phillip. As if she felt that way purposely to slight him.

He took a step closer. "I've been the perfect gentleman." He cocked his head to one side. "But perhaps it's not gentlemen that you like."

He grabbed her upper arms and pulled her toward him. He leaned in. Francesca watched incredulously as his face grew closer. She turned her face just in time and his lips landed on her jawline.

She jerked her head back.

His face flushed with anger or embarrassment. The color spread down his neck. His fingers dug harder into her upper arms, hurting her.

Fear spiked through Francesca, but then with a familiar snap, fear transformed into anger. Outrage and white-hot heat seared through her. She didn't care if he was offended, how big he was, or who his family was. She wrenched her right arm free.

Burckhardt slid his hand around her waist and pulled her roughly against him.

Francesca bent back and reached for the fire iron beside the fireplace behind her. Her groping fingers found the handle. She shoved the poker between them raking his front and smearing black soot across his fencing whites from hip to chest. He released her, and she pushed him backwards with the poker tip against his chest.

He took two steps back, brushed at the soot and smeared it further. "You little ... How dare you." His teeth set and eyes narrowed.

"Shall we see how *you* like a scratched face?" Francesca flicked the tip of the iron upwards. He flinched back.

It wasn't a sword, but the weight of the black iron felt good in her hands.

He reached for it, but she feinted, dropping the tip beneath and around his hand and back up toward his face again.

She advanced and he retreated. Fire seared through her veins. She felt powerful, dangerous.

He shook his head. "You stupid girl." He tried again to grab the poker.

She corkscrewed the point around his hand in a perfect double-disengage. She advanced again and he backed away. A triumphant thrill ran through her.

When they reached the crutches, Francesca gathered them up with her free hand. She tossed the iron, which spun through the air towards Burckhardt. She ran from the room as he caught it.

Anger and triumph burned as she hurried down the stairs. *How dare he!* She glanced back. She almost wished he would follow her so she could give him another piece of her mind, but he didn't.

Francesca's exaltation and anger cooled as she and the signora helped Sebi to his room and into bed, propping up his injured leg.

Clearer headed now, she considered what had happened. She'd made an enemy of Burckhardt—that was certain. She'd insulted him by rejecting him and he wouldn't abide insults. Well so be it. Perhaps he would have been content with a kiss, but how could she have been sure? Even so, she wouldn't have given him one. She rubbed her aching upper arms. She'd likely have bruises there soon.

She debated who she should tell about Burckhardt's actions. Papa was gone. Sebi would not be much use in his current condition. Signor Gallo had taken to his bed earlier in the day with a toothache. Francesca didn't know Maestro Ferro well enough to want to confide in him, and if she told Signora Bianchi, she would only watch *her* that much closer. Antonio was a possibility. But he would probably tell Maestro Ferro who would, in all likelihood, speak with the signora.

Should she tell them at all? She remembered Viola who was sent away because of her relationship with Antonio. There had been others as well who had gotten involved with one of the students. Whenever there was an impropriety of any sort, the girl always seemed to be the one who was forced to leave. Would it be different for the maestro's daughter? She couldn't be sure and wasn't willing to take the risk. Anyway, she wasn't afraid of Burckhardt. She'd proven that today.

At the very least, she would tell Catalina and warn Phillip that Burckhardt had it in for him, if he hadn't figured that out already.

"I should have listened to you," Phillip said from the top of the cellar steps with an apologetic look. "I might have won."

The sight of him made Francesca's pulse flutter. Standing in the candlelight below with their foils, she shook her head. "I'm just glad he didn't hurt you."

"You and me both." Phillip descended the stairs.

"It's my fault," she said.

He scowled as he stopped in front of her. "How do you figure that?"

"He told me. He said he wanted to scratch up your face so I wouldn't like you anymore."

He watched her with a hint of a smile. "And would that work?"

She shook her head. "Of course not. I wouldn't care if…" she trailed off when she saw his mischievous grin.

"So, you're saying you fancy me?"

"I, well, I." Her cheeks burned. "I'm saying *he* fancies *me*."

Phillip's grin remained. "At last, some glimmer of intelligence from the heir to the Ernst fortune."

The heat in her cheeks spread up to her hairline. "Are you saying *you* fancy me?" she teased back. She thought perhaps he blushed too.

Then she remembered how close Burckhardt had come to blinding

Phillip in one eye. "Please, Phillip, you must be careful. I don't think I could stand it if Burckhardt hurt you because of me."

His grin faded. "He does bear watching. I don't know how someone so big can be such a little worm."

Francesca rubbed her bruised upper arm with her free hand. She still felt Burckhardt's fingers there. Anger crept into her voice. "I think that's unfair to worms."

He laughed as he took his foil from her. "Perhaps some drills in *Prima guard* are in order. I may need to protect my head again."

She nodded and took her *en garde* position.

"But first," Phillip said. "By way of an apology for not listening to you, let's fence."

She gasped. "Truly?"

"Of course," Phillip grinned. "You've earned it. Just watch out for my pretty face."

Francesca chuckled as she faced off against him. Her heart pounded in her ears and blood roared through her veins. All else fell away but her, her sword, and Phillip.

He called, "Fence!"

This time, instead of attacking like she had tried to do with Sebi, Francesca retreated. She calmed her nerves and waited for Phillip to attack. She inched forward then backed away as she played with the distance between them. He was taller so he had longer reach. She needed to sneak in close to be able to hit him. She advanced quickly and—

"What goes on here!"

Francesca stumbled into Phillip as they both turned toward the top of the stairs.

The Turtle stood on the top step, a nightcap on his bald head and one side of his face swollen. He held a gray wool blanket around his shoulders and his hairy shins showed beneath the hem of his nightshirt. He stretched his neck out and back in, stomped a slippered foot, and roared again.

"What goes on here?"

CHAPTER 10
CONSEQUENCES

Francesca and Phillip hid their blades behind their backs, but it was too late.

Panic coursed through her, and she fought the urge to bolt. There was nowhere to go. Her stomach rose and for a moment she thought she might throw up.

"Good evening, Signor Gallo," she said in her most innocent voice. "I, well, I couldn't sleep so I came down and happened to—"

"Do you take me for an idiot?" Signor Gallo stomped down the stairs and faced Francesca.

"No, signore." She dropped her eyes.

His red face seethed. His left cheek was swollen, and his breath made her rock back.

He put a hand to his distended cheek as he hissed. "Does your father's absence give you leave to act like a common harlot?"

Her cheeks flamed, and her anger rose. "I di—"

A gasp cut her off, as the signore grabbed her bruised upper arm.

He hauled her towards the stairs. "This is outrageous!"

He paused long enough to say to Phillip in English, "Go to your room and await your punishment."

"It's my fault," she said. "You needn't punish him."

The Turtle didn't answer. He pulled her on, through the kitchen and great hall—where she got one last look at Phillip's stricken face—then up the stairs and on to the signora's room. He banged on her door.

Francesca cringed.

Signora Bianchi's muffled voice called, "Just a moment." She answered the door breathless, her string-bean frame wrapped in a gray shawl over her pale-blue nightgown, and her usually severe hair disheveled. "What's happened?"

Signor Gallo waved both hands at Francesca. "I caught this one fencing in the cellar with Lord Worthington!"

Signora Bianchi drew in a breath and put her hand to her mouth. "Dear Lord in heaven." She closed her eyes and leaned against the door frame.

"Well?" demanded Signor Gallo. "What are you going to do about it?"

Francesca expected her governess to go red in the face and yell as she usually did when she misbehaved. Instead, the signora's hands fluttered about her face like butterflies afraid to land, and tears filled her eyes. Her silence frightened Francesca more than all the shouting in the world. Dread spread through her gut.

"I'll see to it," Signora Bianchi said quietly. She opened her door and drew Francesca inside.

"Such behavior cannot be tolerated," the Turtle said. He stretched his neck out and pulled it in.

"I'm keenly aware." Signora Bianchi blinked back tears. "Thank you, signore." She began to ease the door closed.

The Turtle stopped the door with his fingers. "When you've dealt with the girl, I could use your medical expertise for my tooth. It's become unbearable."

The signora nodded. "As soon as I'm able." Then she closed the door.

A single candle lit the simple room. An oak armoire took up one corner. A wooden crucifix and a mirror above a small writing desk were the only ornaments.

The signora took Francesca's hand and sat on the bed. She wiped at her long face before she spoke.

"I'm sorry, Franny," she said.

She had never, ever, called her Franny. Only Catalina called her that. "I'm afraid I've failed you."

"What do you mean?" A pit opened in Francesca's stomach. "It's not your fault. I'm the one who misbehaved."

Signora Bianchi shook her head and laid a hand on Francesca's cheek. "No dear, what I mean is that Signor Gallo is right, this sort of conduct cannot be tolerated. Drastic action must be taken. I've no choice but to take you to San Ludovico a Colleviti."

The convent! The blood drained from Francesca's body. She sank to the bed next to Signora Bianchi, her legs weak. Her voice trembled. "You'd send me away? From here? Forever?"

Signora Bianchi wiped her cheek. "It's for the best. I'm sorry. I failed in my responsibility to instill some sense of propriety in you. I should have been firmer, tried harder."

"But…" Cold fear curled upward from Francesca's stomach. "Papa would never allow it."

"Your father gave me full authority before he left. Though God knows how hard it will be for him when he returns. He loves you so. And I know how much you remind him of your mother."

Panic followed the fear. If Nana were alive, she would side with Francesca, but Nana was gone too. Her breath came in quick gasps. She'd counted on the fact that Papa loved her too much to send her away. It hadn't occurred to her that she might be sent away without his knowledge. Once she was gone, would he try to get her back?

She slid to her knees in front of Signora Bianchi as sobs ripped from her. She put her head in the signora's lap. "Please don't send me away. Please! Please! I'd die in that place! Please."

Her governess laid a thin hand on Francesca's shuddering shoulders.

"I promise I'll never touch a sword again. Never. I'll never even *think* about fencing. Please, just don't send me there!"

"You've left me no choice."

She looked up at her governess as she wiped at her eyes and nose. "Punish me any way you like. I'll do whatever you ask. Please."

Signora Bianchi hesitated. A frown creased her forehead as she looked down at Francesca's tearstained face.

"Please," Francesca whispered.

Signora Bianchi took a deep breath and looked away. "It's very late and I need to see to Signor Gallo's tooth. There's no more to be done tonight. We'll discuss this further in the morning."

The signora tied on a robe, collected her medical bag from the armoire, and led Francesca to her room.

As the door closed behind her, Francesca heard a key rattle in the lock. She fought down panic. She'd never been locked in before.

She paced the room, too worried to sleep.

Her older cousin Lucia had been forced into the convent of San Ludovico a Colleviti. Lucia had been strong and daring and Francesca had looked up to her. She even jumped her horse and rode astride when she went fox hunting with her brothers. Her father had called her 'willful' and 'defiant' and had sent her away.

Two years at the convent turned Lucia into someone Francesca couldn't recognize. Now she barely spoke above a whisper and wouldn't meet anyone's eyes. The idea of being trapped there herself made Francesca nauseous.

She paced some more, back and forth. Back and forth.

She needed to think, to come up with a plan. She paced faster and with more determination. There had to be a way out.

Francesca was not exactly sure which was the greater sin she had committed, being caught alone with a boy, or fencing. The two together, well, that was apparently unforgivable. The assumption seemed to be that this had happened more than once. What if she convinced them she had only fenced once? Maybe her sentence would be more lenient. Even if she couldn't save herself, at least they might not expel Phillip.

She thought of her plump fencing mannequin under the bed. That would be proof of her guilt if the signora searched her room. She dragged it out and disemboweled it. She hid the stockings and fencing jacket among her dirty clothes in the armoire. Her fencing books she wedged under the thick vines and leaves of the bougainvillea outside her window.

She tried to recall her conversation with her governess. Had she admitted to fencing more than once? She didn't think so. Had they already questioned Phillip? He would need to tell the same story, but how could she let him know?

She remembered Sebi's leg wound. He was probably in bed right next door. She went to the wall adjoining Sebi's room and knocked. "Sebi! Sebi! Can you hear me?"

She tried twice more before she got a surly, muffled answer. "Damn it, it's the middle of the night."

"Please, I need to talk to you!"

"If you want to talk to me, come here."

"I can't! I'm locked in!"

"Now what have you done?"

"Please, Sebi, I need your help!"

She couldn't catch his reply, just the groan that accompanied it.

She paced impatiently until his voice came more clearly from the other side of her door. "So, what's happened?"

She pressed up against the door. "Just listen, Sebi. The Turtle caught me and Phillip fencing in the cellar—"

"I should have known you wouldn't give it up."

"Please, Sebi, they're going to send me to Colleviti unless you help me."

"Lord Almighty, now you've done it!"

"You have to get word to Phillip to tell them this was the first and only time we fenced. That we met in the kitchen by accident."

There was a long pause. Francesca pressed her forehead hard against the oak of the door and squeezed her eyes shut. "Please, Sebi!"

"All right," Sebi said. "I'll see what I can do." Then he chuckled. "But I'm not doing it for you. I'm doing it for the nuns. You'd be a bad influence." After a moment he said, "Good luck." Then she heard him crutch away. She went back to pacing.

As the sky outside her window lightened, she heard a commotion near the stable. She rushed to the window.

The stable hands pushed Papa's carriage out and hooked up a pair of chestnut horses. Francesca shivered and gulped back a lump in her throat. The driver climbed aboard, and the carriage rattled into the courtyard.

Francesca had never been much for prayer, but she knelt, hands clasped on her bedspread. "Please God, I'd be a horrible nun. Please don't take me. I promise I'll be honorable. I'll never break a promise again." The words Papa taught the students came to her and she repeated them over and over, like a rosary. "To defend God and country. To keep one's word. To defend the weak and innocent. To never abandon a noble cause. To avoid lying and cheating. To exhibit courage in word and deed. To live for freedom, justice, and all that is good. To die with honor."

She was still reciting when she heard the signora's footsteps along with an unfamiliar set in the hall. She rose and faced the door. There was a hasty knock, a rattle as the door was unlocked, and Signora Bianchi and Maestro Ferro entered.

The signora looked bone tired, her face drawn and deep circles under her eyes. The maestro's high cheekbones each held a patch of pink and he pulled nervously at his cuffs.

Francesca dropped her head, cast her eyes down, and looked penitent.

"Come along, Francesca," Signora Bianchi said. "It's time to go."

Fear exploded in Francesca's belly. She backed away shaking her head. "Where?" she whispered.

"You know where," the signora said. "Come along. Catalina will pack a few things for you."

"I can't. I won't!" her voice trembled. "Papa would never allow it."

"You will," insisted her governess, through tight jaws. "Do you think this is what I want? Catalina and I will have to leave as well. This is our home, too. You brought this on all of us."

"No!" Francesca pressed up against the far wall. *It's all my fault. I've ruined everything.*

The signora motioned the maestro toward Francesca. "If you please."

The maestro took a step forward and tugged at his collar, his blush deepening. "Please, signorina, we mustn't make a scene."

A scene! She was being sent to prison, possibly for life, and he was worried about a scene. Her breath came in gasps and her vision started to narrow. She'd never felt so trapped.

The maestro drew near and offered her his arm.

Francesca slid away along the wall.

"Maestro," Signora Bianchi said, "You have my permission to carry her if she will not walk."

Maestro Ferro gave a small grimace, but Francesca got the message. The signora had a whole salle of men at her command. Who could Francesca count on? Sebi perhaps, Catalina, and Phillip who might well be under lock and key.

Her hand trembled as she took the maestro's arm. As she walked down the hall tears filled her eyes and blurred her world, the nearly forgotten imps from her recurring nightmare scurrying along the walls.

Somehow Francesca managed to reach the foot of the stairs. At the end of the entry hall the double doors of the salle stood open. The red and black carriage waited beyond. Her legs felt leaden. At least if she were walking to the gallows her misery would be over soon. This was far worse.

With the maestro and signora on either side of her, and the signora's arm around her waist, she moved toward the doors.

"Please don't make me go," she whispered.

"It's for your own good. I only want what's best for you," Signora Bianchi said. "The nuns will do what I could not."

When they reached the double doors, Francesca drew back gasping for air. There were students scattered about the courtyard, probably trying to figure out what was going on. She looked around for Catalina but couldn't see her.

"May I at least say goodbye to Catalina and Sebi?" she managed between gulps of air. "Where's Antonio?"

"They will come visit," the signora said as she propelled her forward.

"What about Achilles? Can I at least see him?" Would anyone else even miss her? She wanted to bolt, to fling herself on Achilles' back and flee, but where would she go?

"No, Francesca."

She stepped into the sunshine and squinted at the dazzling glare in her tear-filled eyes. The carriage driver straightened and opened the door. As Francesca stepped up to it, she wiped her eyes with her sleeve. Through the carriage window opposite she saw Burckhardt on the far side of the courtyard. He was laughing at her.

Laughing! Suddenly the world gave a twist, and she saw the way out.

She put her hands on either side of the carriage door and stiffened her arms as the signora tried to push her inside.

"Francesca, this is foolish," Signora Bianchi said.

She spun on her governess. Heat suffused her. She realized for the first time that she was taller than Signora Bianchi, and much stronger. The signora seemed small and fragile.

Maestro Ferro stood a step behind the signora nervously smoothing his goatee. Francesca kept her voice low, but she didn't hide her intensity. "Yes, I was foolish. I was wrong to fence, I know. But I only did it so that I could defend myself if Lord Ernst tried to have his way with me again!"

"Lord Ernst!" said the signora and signore together as they took a half step back.

Francesca crowed with fierce delight inside but kept her face sober. She scanned the silent and still courtyard. Had anyone else besides the driver heard her words, or had they only heard the maestro and signora gasp Burckhardt's name? She couldn't see Burckhardt behind her, but she could see others' eyes going to him.

The signora stared at Francesca. Suspicion and concern chased across her face, which made her eyebrows dance. After a few seconds the maestro glanced around the courtyard and then cleared his throat. "Perhaps we should discuss this inside."

"That might be best," the signora said. She took Francesca's arm and led her quickly back into the salle.

Francesca's entire body unclenched as she moved away from the carriage. The world swam and she tripped on the step up to the doorway. She shook her head to clear her mind. She needed to get this just right.

Signora Bianchi ushered her and the maestro into the family's private parlor and closed the door behind them. She turned to Francesca. "Do you know what you're saying?" she asked.

She nodded. Accusing a nobleman of attempted rape was no small matter and would make Burckhardt an even more formidable enemy. But better that than life in prison.

She told them about the events after Sebi's injury without embellishment, though she omitted Burckhardt's jealousy. When she explained about the fireplace poker, the signora and maestro exchanged a look. Could they have seen Burckhardt's smudged clothes? The maestro stepped out for a few minutes so Francesca could show the signora the bruises on her upper arms.

"So," Francesca concluded when the maestro returned, "when I met Lord Worthington by chance in the kitchen, and he told me about his maestro's secret fencing moves, I thought knowing them might be advantageous if Lord Ernst made further advances. I tricked Lord Worthington into showing me. You see, I'm to blame."

The signore and signora stared at her, stunned.

"You planned on dueling with Lord Ernst?" the maestro said, incredulously.

"Of course not," Francesca said. "I just wanted to defend my honor."

Signora Bianchi said, not unkindly, "Why didn't you come to me and tell me what happened?"

"Well," Francesca said. "Sebi had been stabbed and Signor Gallo was ill. They needed you. Besides," she looked away. "I didn't think you'd believe me. It's my word against his, and he's related to the King of Prussia."

Her governess sat heavily in a damask armchair. "I would have believed you, Francesca. I'm sorry you didn't trust me."

"I take it there were no other witnesses to Lord Ernst's ... liberties," the maestro said.

Francesca shook her head.

"Unfortunate," Maestro Ferro said to Signora Bianchi. "He'll deny everything, of course. It will be her word against his."

Fierce anger flared through Francesca. "It's not fair," she nearly shouted, "you tell me I must preserve my honor, but when I try to learn how, I'm punished! Why must a girl be weak and helpless? Why must she wait to be rescued by a man? What if I hadn't picked up that fire iron? What would have become of me if I hadn't rescued myself? What's so wrong with a woman fencing? It's maddening!"

Francesca railed a while longer, while the maestro fidgeted uncomfortably, and her governess waited for her to finish.

When she fell quiet, Signora Bianchi said softly, "Francesca, it's your willfulness and your utter disregard for propriety that cannot be tolerated. And fencing? Good Lord, no man will marry a woman with a sword. No man wants his courage or skill compared to that of his wife. You would die unloved and childless."

The look of conviction and pain on her governess' face drove the anger out of her. She saw with sudden clarity how lonely the signora was and how much she wished to spare Francesca that loneliness. She honestly believed she would be helping her if she locked her away.

Francesca thought of her feelings for Phillip, and that moment in the dark, her longing. Was that her choice? Fencing or love, but never both? How could she make that choice? But then, it had already been made for her.

She felt sorry for the signora. She seemed so small, and so very unhappy, but she held Francesca's fate in her hands. Francesca couldn't bring herself to ask if she was still bound for the convent. She was too afraid to hear the answer.

Finally, the maestro shifted and said, "I shall have strong words with Lord Ernst, but without corroboration..." he gave a small, helpless shrug. "We must keep a close watch on him." He turned to Francesca. "And Lord Worthington?"

"He's been a perfect gentleman," Francesca said. "I'm sorry I tricked him. Please don't expel him over my foolishness."

"I don't think that will be necessary," Maestro Ferro said as his shoulders relaxed.

"So..." Francesca said in a small voice to Signora Bianchi.

The signora took a deep breath and exhaled slowly. "I may have been hasty in my decision. But you were both out of bed after hours. There will be punishment. Whatever possessed you, Francesca?"

Francesca's stomach unknotted. She considered her answer. She was not above playing the sympathy card. "Well, after what happened with Lord Ernst, I had nightmares. I couldn't sleep. Nana used to make me warm milk when I had bad dreams, and I missed her. I thought some warm milk might help."

The signora rose and straightened her dress. "Well, bad dreams or not, you will not leave your room at night. Not unless the villa is on fire. And I will hold you to your promise to never touch a blade again." She opened the door to the parlor. "Go to your room while we decide what's to be done. I'll have breakfast brought up."

Francesca heaved a sigh as she climbed the steps. She'd done it. Phillip was safe from expulsion, safe to learn how to defeat his sworn enemy, and she was safe from the convent, at least for now.

A servant brought her a plate of boiled eggs, cheese, and dried apples. Francesca attacked the food with vigor and then collapsed back onto her bed. As she fell asleep, she thought, *thank you, Lord, this time I'll give it up for good. I'll never think or talk about fencing ever again. I swear.*

She fell asleep in moments. There was no nightmare, no drowning in dark water. She dreamed she was fencing with Papa, and winning.

CHAPTER 11
NOTHING INSIDE

Francesca scaled the stairs to her bedroom. Never had two flights seemed so long. Her back, feet, and hands ached. Even her bones felt tired.

Signora Bianchi had taken her at her word when she said she would do anything as punishment. 'Anything', in this case, meant collecting and chopping vegetables, plucking chickens, churning milk, and scouring pans. But instead of all afternoon, like before, she was assigned all day. The salle fed more than fifty people, three times a day, so work didn't stop from dawn to dusk. The first week of her three-week sentence was nearly up.

Francesca stopped when she reached the top of the stairs and arched her back, which cracked in three places. She groaned. Still, anything was better than the convent.

Sebastian's door opened and he limped into the hallway. When he saw her, he hid his limp, but the pain was clear in the tightness of his jaw when he took a few steps toward her.

"Have you seen Catalina?" he asked.

Francesca shook her head. Even that took effort. "No, I've been in the kitchen all day. Any news?"

Sebi ran a hand through his hair and grabbed the back of his neck. "No, and it's worrying us."

Papa had agreed to write to Catalina's parents about a match between Sebi and Catalina, but there was no way to know if or when Papa had sent a letter, if it had arrived safely, or what Catalina's parents might do.

Francesca tried to sound hopeful when she replied, "No news is better than bad news."

"Not by much," Sebi said as he headed for the stairs.

She watched him limp away, wishing again that she could help them. But she couldn't change national policies or find new silk markets. Though after church last week, she'd convinced their priest to buy new silk vestments and altar cloths for the parish—for whatever good that would do.

If she at least knew who Catalina's father had approached about marrying her, then she could try to influence their decision, but they didn't even know that. And while she and Catalina had spent late evenings hidden from the signora theorizing who it might be, they'd come no closer to an answer.

Francesca stopped at the threshold of her room—or her torture chamber. The nightmares were back, worse than ever, so she'd mostly given up on sleep. She was still required to be in her room from dusk to dawn, however.

She entered, closed the door, knelt beside her bed, and felt beneath it. She knew they wouldn't be there. Signor Gallo had taken her foil, and she had disposed of her mannequin and books, but she had to check.

Good, she told herself. *Less temptation that way.* But she missed them. She would not fence, not after the vow she'd made. She just needed to touch the things from that old life. Of course, even touching them would break her vow not to think about fencing ever again. But how was she supposed to stop thinking? She rubbed her face with both hands.

Francesca went to the window and scanned the courtyard for a glimpse of Phillip. She missed his clipped English accent, the way he tilted his head when he laughed, his blue eyes and beautiful smile. The few times she'd seen him had been gold shards in a world of gray.

Her eyes drifted to the stable where Phillip served his sentence mucking out the stalls in his off hours, but she saw no sign of him. She hoped Achilles was being exercised well since the stables were now off limits to her. Yet more for her to miss.

As the light faded, she noticed Burckhardt shove one of the younger boys. As far as she knew, all Burckhardt had suffered was a split lip, probably from either Sebastian or Antonio—since if they hadn't done it, she would have heard them discuss who had at dinner.

She sat down at her desk and grabbed paper and her inkwell. She and

Catalina might not know who her parents had contacted about marrying Catalina, but Catalina's mother did. Just maybe she could convince her to tell them. After all, she had promised not to mention Sebi and Catalina, she hadn't promised not to make any other enquiries.

When she finished, Francesca folded the letter and set it aside. She looked around her room and groaned. She took the book she had borrowed from Papa's private library, *Travels into Africa*, off her shelf. She sat on her bed but stared at a page without reading it. The world of adventures seemed farther away than ever.

She felt her nightmare now, even in the daylight. Each day the doors and windows faded away a little more and the water rose. Each morning it was a little harder to move and breathe. Someday soon the creatures would come, and she would drown.

———┼———

While Francesca mended one of Antonio's shirts, the clank of blades and cheers of students filtered in through the window. She had closed it, but still the sound came in. She sat with her back to the window so she wouldn't be tempted to look. She mumbled to herself, "To avoid lying and cheating. To exhibit courage in word and deed."

Out of the corner of her eye she could see Catalina glance at her periodically with pinched eyebrows. Francesca wished she'd stop it. She'd had that same expression for weeks—ever since Francesca finished her kitchen sentence and Signora Bianchi had insisted that Catalina stay close in case Burckhardt tried to get her alone again.

That was also when she'd received a reply from Catalina's mother. She sweetly stated how happy she was that Francesca and Catalina had become such good friends, but pointedly ignored the question about the match. Another dead end.

"To live for freedom, justice, and all that is good," Francesca mumbled on. She'd kept her promise not to fence, but she'd also vowed not to think about fencing. That was the hard part. The more she tried not to, the more it burst into her mind. She repeated Papa's code of honor over and over. The louder her thoughts, the more she repeated the code, until she mumbled out loud.

At least she no longer tried to catch glimpses of Phillip. Not since last week when she caught sight of him on the way to Latin lessons. He had looked thoroughly miserable, which only made her feel worse and reminded her that she'd never be allowed to talk to him again.

Catalina set down her mending and perched on the arm of Francesca's chair. "You look tired."

"I'm fine." That was oddly true. It had been a month, and she'd settled into a gray numbness that nothing seemed to penetrate. She hovered there, as if between sleep and waking. She didn't feel horrible. She didn't feel anything at all.

Catalina gave a skeptical huff. Francesca glanced up at her and Catalina looked away. "Signora Salucci's little ones have the chicken pox and I told her we'd come take care of them."

"Fine." Francesca folded up her sewing.

"Fine?" Catalina's voice rose. "Fine? No excuses? No arguments? You're not angry with me for volunteering you without your permission?"

"No, it's fine," Francesca said blankly. Really, what did it matter? She set aside the sewing and rose.

Catalina frowned. "Never mind the fact that you've never had chicken pox and could die."

Francesca looked away. "I'm sure it will be—"

"Fine?" Catalina crossed her arms and plopped into another chair.

"Are we going?" Francesca motioned toward the door.

"No," Catalina said. "The children are ... fine."

Francesca sat and resumed work on the shirt. "Then why did you say they were sick?"

"Well, I wanted to make you angry. For heaven's sake Francesca, it's been like living with a ghost these last few weeks!"

She wasn't angry anymore, ever, which she supposed was good. She wasn't happy either, or sad, or anything. "I'm not angry."

"*I know*, Franny, that's the problem."

Signora Bianchi entered and set down a stack of cloth napkins with loose hems. Francesca tied off her thread, folded the shirt, set it aside, and picked up a napkin.

"They don't all need to be done today," the signora said.

Francesca looked up and saw a concerned look pass between the signora and Catalina. Francesca thought vaguely that she should be angry at her governess. She was doing everything the signora asked. She was being precisely what the signora had demanded she be for years. She was obedient, quiet, and if not exactly cheerful, she was at least uncomplaining. The signora still wasn't happy, but really, she couldn't be bothered to be cross with her.

"Well, Francesca," Signora Bianchi said. "Is there anything you'd like to do today?"

Francesca was surprised. The signora had never asked that question before. Then her mind went places it shouldn't. She struggled to keep her mind blank, to keep from thinking of *him* and *it*. She folded her hands in her lap and started the litany again in her mind. "No, signora. I'm fine."

Catalina handed Francesca yet another bucket of near boiling water and Francesca poured it over the ash-covered bucking cloth which covered a large wooden vat of laundry. She watched the water sink through the cloth.

It was a hot day, and between that and the boiling water in the vat, sweat dripped from her temples and ran off the tip of her nose. Her shoulders and back ached from hauling water and stirring laundry, and the acrid smell of lye, ash, and urine burnt the inside of her nose—but the sensations were distant, as if those things were happening to someone else.

The tub was set up out-of-doors between the servants' quarters and the kitchen gardens. Francesca and Catalina were supposed to be learning the complicated bucking, or whitening, process. They'd been through most of the procedure, but the steps blended together in Francesca's mind, like most things did these days.

"That's enough, Francesca," Signora Bianchi said. "Now it must sit overnight."

"Yes, signora." She handed the bucket to Maria, one of the laundry maids, a stout girl whose shoulders rippled with muscle from handling wet linens. Catalina asked a few questions while Francesca wiped the sweat from her eyes and waited for the next task the signora would assign her.

"The process will be repeated tomorrow and after rinsing, the laundry will be laid in the sun to dry," the signora said.

"Yes, signora."

Her governess paused, then sighed. "Francesca, do you realize that the only words you've said to me in the last three days are 'Yes, signora?'"

She opened her mouth, then closed it.

Signora Bianchi watched her a moment, then said, "Come along then, it's time for your history lesson."

She and Catalina followed their governess back toward the salle. Francesca kept her eyes down as they passed the great hall where the students were at lunch. A stray scent of ham from the dining room took Francesca's mind back to the ham curing in the cellar, to *him*, and *it*. *To defend God and country. To keep one's word.*

As they climbed the stairs the signora said, "Francesca, is there anything you wish to discuss?"

"No, signora."

Signora Bianchi stopped outside the schoolroom, motioned Catalina inside, and studied Francesca's face.

"Have I done something wrong?" asked Francesca.

"No. I want," she paused a moment. "I had hoped, when you finally settled down, that you'd take more of an interest. And look at you. You're not eating. You've become all skin and bones."

"Yes, signora."

Her governess huffed.

"I'll try to eat more."

"Do." Then her voice softened. "And, I'd like you to smile now and again."

Francesca raised the corners of her mouth. The signora gave her a pained smile in return. "That will be all."

She turned toward the schoolroom where Catalina watched her, worry etched over her face. Francesca wished she'd stop it.

"Francesca," called her governess.

She turned back to face her.

"I give you permission to go for a ride after class. I'll speak with Cassio. Just be back in time for dinner."

"Yes, signora."

———†———

Achilles' whinnies echoed as she entered the stable. He reared and tossed his head so violently that she hurried to his stall to calm him. He nearly bowled her over in his efforts to nuzzle her face and neck. His big rubbery tongue slurped up her cheek. She laughed for the first time in what seemed like forever and wrapped her arms around his neck. He rumbled deep in his chest like a huge cat purring.

She held on to him as he calmed, and she felt as if a thread in the gray mantle that covered her had parted. She tried to count the days since she'd seen Achilles, but they all blended into a formless mass. Two months maybe? She had no idea of the date. Was it August or September?

"It's a pleasure to see you, mistress, to be sure," Cassio said behind her.

She turned and smiled at him, almost a real smile. His mop of white hair and his tanned and lined face were comforting.

"The big lad has missed you something fierce. We all have." Cassio held his tan cap and fingered the brim.

Francesca scratched Achilles' jowls and he shook his head with pleasure. "I've missed all of you too."

"I'll get him saddled in a jiffy," Cassio said, lifting her sidesaddle onto Achilles' back. "Your young man, Lord Worthington, was a great help. He has a real feel for the horses. He's a good lad."

Her young man. No one, besides Antonio and Sebi at dinner, had spoken his name in her hearing in weeks. The events of that night and day were supposed to be a dead secret, and therefore, the whole salle probably knew. She glanced four stalls down to where Iago munched some oats. She tried not to think about their race through the olive grove.

"Is Lord Worthington all right?" she asked.

"I wouldn't go so far as to say, 'all right.' He's been as forlorn as a mare without her colt, but I don't think he found his time here too burdensome."

Francesca nodded. That was something at least.

Once on horseback, she directed Achilles across the dueling grounds, behind the barn, and out into the sheep pasture. There she loosened her grip on the reins, and Achilles, cooped-up for far too long, ran.

The warm afternoon sun heated her skin, and the wind flowed through her hair. She lifted and rocked between Achilles' hoof beats, their movements in harmony. The blanket of drab numbness that had smothered her for weeks lifted to reveal a patch of gold sunlight on deep green pasture to her right, a spot of brilliant wildflowers off to her left, the fluffy cream of sheep ahead. Before they reached the far side of the pasture, she noticed that water dripped from her chin. She was sobbing.

When they slowed to a canter on the far side of the pasture, she understood how completely miserable she was and laughed and cried at once. It was lovely to feel something, anything, for a change, even if that something was miserable.

"What am I going to do?" she asked Achilles. "I can't live like this."

He had no answer for her.

They followed a trail into the woods beyond the pasture at a walk, and Francesca reined in when they reached her favorite climbing tree. The massive, gnarled oak had been struck by lightning decades ago. One branch, as large around as Achilles' chest, had partly detached from the force of the blast. The crook of the branch had been burnt black and the outer end slumped to the ground. Now the branch formed a crooked ramp, easily walkable up the rough bark—if she stretched her arms for balance—thirty feet up to the trunk of the tree.

In the past she'd found that ramp irresistible, as attested by the scar just below her elbow. And she had a spot ten feet higher in the branches that she'd worn smooth from hours reading and listening to the wind in the boughs as Achilles cropped grass below.

Today the ramp held no allure, seeming childish and irrelevant. She wished she could go back to those days, before he arrived, before Nana died. Before the specter of Catalina's marriage. She didn't see how, though. Now she had responsibilities she didn't want, sorrows she couldn't avoid, and urges she couldn't satisfy. She nudged Achilles on.

They followed a game trail wherever it led. Here and there the leaves of the underbrush trailed against her skin. The tangy smell of leaf litter and pine resin filled her nose. The trail dipped into a hollow where a small stream trickled, then back up the far side. Moments later she rode out of the woods into a small pasture.

Cotton-puff clouds dotted the sky, and lingering wildflowers freckled the field. To her right stood a crumbling stone barn that had long ago lost its roof and doors—the wood probably taken for other uses. A pile of rubble wrapped in morning glories was all that remained of one corner, and saplings and brush threatened to swallow everything into the forest.

She had forgotten the place existed, though she and Sebi had played there as children, pretending it was a castle that they defended against invading armies. She had no idea who built it or why. She'd asked Papa once and he'd shrugged and guessed that perhaps a previous owner of the villa had pastured cattle nearby.

She directed Achilles through the tan fieldstone shell. *This would be perfect*, said a voice in the back of her mind.

"No! No, it would not," she said aloud.

Achilles tossed his head.

"To defend God and country. To keep one's word. To defend the weak and innocent," she mumbled.

We'd need to move some of the fallen stones out of the way, but that wouldn't be difficult.

"No! I can't," she said to Achilles. "I swore. I swore to the signora and to God. I'd never talk my way out of the convent a second time." A shiver jangled up her spine. "I'd die in that place."

What's the difference, said the voice. *You're already dead.*

"I'm not. I'm not." She tried to convince herself as the gray blanket of numbness settled back onto her.

"To never abandon a noble cause. To avoid lying and cheating. To exhibit courage in word and deed!"

Then the thought stole into her head, *perhaps the convent would be better. At least there would be no temptations there.* She turned Achilles toward home.

———

After that the signora insisted that Francesca go for a ride each day, though she instructed Francesca to take Mateo with her. She referred to it as Francesca's "constitutional," though if it did improve her mood, the improvement was slight.

Francesca made sure to avoid the tumbled-down barn. The thoughts that arose there were forbidden and painful. She rode in the mornings during fencing class so she wouldn't have to hear them in the yard. She mostly ignored Mateo, who grumbled as he followed along.

She had seen little of Burckhardt since the day in the sitting room, and thought of him even less, until one wet day after her ride.

The morning was windy and the weather changeable, though Francesca barely noticed. Dark-bellied clouds chased each other across an open sky. As she rode through the vineyard, a dark cloud swept rain across the landscape. The shower was brief, and she didn't much care if she was wet and was numb to the chill, but Mateo complained and Signora Bianchi would scold, so she headed back.

As she entered the salle, fencing class was being moved indoors. Francesca kept her eyes down as she passed the great hall, but she heard the hubbub of voices and the hollow squeak as wooden tables and benches scraped across the floor as they were pushed out of the way. She climbed the stairs to her room, took off her damp riding jacket, and hung it near the window.

When she opened her door, Burckhardt filled the doorway. He must have followed her up. His pebble eyes were narrowed, and a muscle jumped in his jaw as he stepped forward into the room.

Francesca stepped back. She knew she should be frightened. Fear pressed in at the detachment that surrounded her but couldn't break through.

"You made me a laughingstock," Burckhardt seethed through tight jaws. "You can't imagine what they call me. They say I was beaten by a girl."

Francesca moved sideways to go around him. He grabbed her upper arm and shook her. "I won't be made a fool."

Francesca wished he would shake her hard enough to dislodge the lethargy that clung to her.

He shoved her against the armoire, banging her elbow against the oak, but even the pain couldn't reach her.

"It's time you learned your place," he hissed. Then his bulk was against her, crushing her. He smelled of ham and sweat. His hands were hot where they pinned her arms, fingers digging in. His lips crushed hers against her teeth and she tasted blood, then they moved on toward her jawline.

Fight. Scream. Do something! yelled the voice in her mind. But she couldn't. Hopelessness and helplessness paralyzed her. The door and window disappeared. She was drowning in black water as one huge nightmare creature clawed at her.

His body trapping her, his hands scrabbled at her skirts, and she heard something rip.

Then there was a short, piercing cry and Catalina was there. She hit at Burckhardt's head with her fists and clawed at his face.

Burckhardt raised his arms to block Catalina's attack. Catalina grabbed Francesca's wrist and towed her toward the hallway.

"I'm telling the maestro!" shouted Catalina.

Burckhardt followed them out into the hall, not in the least flustered. "No, you won't."

"I will!" Catalina said, towing Francesca away. "And you'll be—"

"You won't," Burckhardt hissed. "Or I'll say she invited me into her room."

Catalina slowed.

"And I'll say we've been fencing together," he continued. "Her word against mine. I may be sent home, but she'll be sent to the convent."

Catalina wrapped her arms protectively around Francesca. Catalina's whole body shook. "You're a liar and a vile man."

Burckhardt smiled evilly and moved toward them, but the stairs creaked under someone's weight. Burckhardt changed direction and ducked into the schoolroom across the hall. Signor Gallo appeared at the head of the stairs and nodded to the girls as he continued to his room.

Catalina took Francesca's hand, towed her to her own room, and locked the door. Francesca sat on Catalina's bed, drew her legs up, wrapped her arms around them, and rocked. A sea of emotions lapped at her like waves, but she remained above the waterline, and they couldn't touch her.

Catalina paced the room. She used swear words that Francesca had never heard before. Or maybe she made them up. Finally, she stopped and stared at Francesca.

"Say something, Franny! Aren't you angry? Aren't you scared? Don't you even care?"

She dropped her eyes to her knees. "Thank you for rescuing me."

"Arrrrr!" Catalina growled to the ceiling. "The Franny I know wouldn't need to be rescued. The Franny I know would have bitten off his face, clawed his eyes out, and spit in the sockets! I can't take this anymore! You're like a Francesca-shaped doll with nothing inside."

Francesca nodded as tears filled her vision. "That's how I feel, Catalina. When he … I, I hoped he'd kill me."

Catalina's arms enveloped her, and Francesca sobbed on her shoulder for a long time, convulsive, racking sobs. When she quieted Catalina sat back and brushed the hair from Francesca's face.

"We have to fix this, Franny," Catalina said. "I want my friend back and I don't care what it takes. I don't care if we must break every rule in the salle. If you *need* to see Phillip, if you *need* to fence, then that's what we'll do. You can't live like this anymore."

"But I swore!" Francesca stared at the wall and mumbled, "To defend God and country. To keep one's word. To defend the weak and innocent."

"Look at me." Catalina gently turned Francesca's face back to her. "That was before you knew what your oath would cost you. You're not hurting anyone. I don't see how it's any of their affair."

"But I made a bargain. I promised God—"

"God made you this way. He could hardly expect you to be someone else."

Francesca took a deep breath. It felt like the first time in months she'd been able to breathe properly.

"I've watched you nearly kill yourself trying to be someone you're not," Catalina said. "I won't let you do that anymore. I love you too much. And for what? To keep the signora happy? That woman will never be happy."

"Oh, but Catalina, I can't be sent to Colleviti. I can't!"

"Well, then we'll just have to be more clever than the people who would send you there."

CHAPTER 12
ALWAYS

Catalina's words unraveled the blanket of numbness smothering Francesca. Every sensation and every emotion felt new and intense: the brush of the breeze from the open window on her cheek, the softness of Catalina's rose-colored blanket under her hand, Catalina's warm, smooth palm on her arm. She looked around Catalina's bedroom as if seeing it for the first time. She shook off the residual fear from Burckhardt's attack as hope blossomed.

Catalina was right, she was made this way, and God didn't make mistakes. The signora believed a woman with a sword would never find a husband. Well, Phillip didn't seem to mind that she fenced, and even the signora couldn't see the future.

Francesca hugged Catalina and wiped at the tears drying on her cheeks. "What would I ever do without you?"

"The better question is what are we to do about Burckhardt?" Catalina said as her brow furrowed.

Francesca considered. "Well, when Papa gets home, he'll believe me, not Burckhardt. He'll know what to do. In the meantime, perhaps we can't tell Maestro Ferro or it will come down to Burkhardt's word against mine, but we can tell Sebi and Antonio."

Catalina nodded. "They'll make him think twice about ever coming near you again. I'll talk to the house servants as well. If they see him anywhere

107

he's not supposed to be, they can tell your brothers or Maestro Ferro immediately."

"Thank you," said Francesca. "And maybe they won't let me walk around with a sword, but that doesn't mean I have to be completely unarmed. I'll borrow a paring knife from the kitchen."

"Speaking of swords" Catalina said.

Gloom settled over Francesca. "Phillip must hate me for getting him in trouble. Even if he was willing to fence with me again, which I doubt, how am I to work it out? I'm not allowed to speak to him."

Catalina rolled her eyes. "Of course he'd be willing," she said. "You haven't seen him, Franny. He's moped around just as much as you.

"Truly?" The idea that Phillip had missed her too sent a tingle of heat along her skin.

"And I'm not forbidden to talk to him," Catalina said. "Tell me what you want me to say. I can catch him on his way to his Italian lesson tonight."

Francesca's mind flew to the tumbled-down barn. It would be perfect, *if* he was willing to take the risk. Her heart raced and the heat intensified in her cheeks. She put her hands to her face.

"Poor Franny," Catalina pulled a face. "I never thought I'd see *you* lovesick."

Francesca grabbed the pillow and swatted her. They laughed.

Francesca rode Achilles to her favorite climbing tree. As she looked around for Phillip, her stomach fluttered. Phillip was to come on foot to meet here and they would go on together to the old barn. Four days had passed since they'd arranged the meeting. Waiting for this moment had made those days seem endless.

Too nervous to sit, she dismounted and hopped up on the massive fallen tree limb. Balancing carefully, she walked the rough-barked ramp up to where lightning had struck, twenty-some feet up the trunk of the old oak. She sat down in the V left when the branch had partly detached. Her legs dangled as she ran her fingers over the familiar black scorch marks.

Is he coming? She worried. *What if he changed his mind? What if he doesn't want to see me?*

The whole thing had been easy enough to arrange. The signora insisted she ride regularly "to keep her spirits up." Francesca arranged to ride in the late afternoons, once her lessons and tasks were finished for the day. Phillip would be free at that time as well, at least a few days a week.

Francesca was still required to bring Mateo, but for a bribe of sweets or a coin or two he was more than happy to ride, or nap, elsewhere and keep his mouth shut. She would meet up with him on the way back, and no one would be the wiser.

Francesca hadn't seen Phillip, but according to Catalina, when she told him the plan, he seemed more relieved than anything.

Where was he? There was so much she needed to say.

The underbrush rustled. Both she and Achilles turned to look.

There he was, more golden, lithe, and handsome than she remembered. Lightning shot through her as though the tree were struck again. She wanted to call out. She wanted to say a million things at once, but they all clogged her throat.

Phillip went to Achilles, then turned and scanned the area. His eyes found hers. Neither spoke for a long moment.

Then Phillip laughed. "I had planned a whole speech," he said. "But now I can't remember any of it."

"Was it a good speech?" she asked. She wanted her arms around him, but she shook too much at the moment to risk the descent. Why had she climbed the stupid tree?

"A very good speech."

"Can you tell me the main points?"

He gave her a lopsided smile. "I missed you."

Her heart sang and her nervousness disappeared. "That's an excellent speech. I missed you too."

"Shall I come up, or are you coming down?"

"I'll come down." She stood and stretched out her arms for balance.

Phillip watched her descend. "My God, Francesca. You are fearless."

She paused mid-branch and tipped her head to one side. "No. I've plenty of fears. I just enjoy being afraid."

He shook his head. "You are a singular girl."

When she reached the bottom, he took her hand. "My lady," he said as she hopped off the branch. He kept hold of her hand as she faced him.

"I'm sorry for the trouble I caused you." She looked into his blue eyes.

"Don't be," he said. "It was worth it. Besides, I enjoyed working in the stable. Cassio has become a friend, the best I've found here, other than you. He's been more like a father to me than my own."

"You never speak of your father." Francesca thought of what Burckhardt had called him—a drunkard and a rogue.

"That's because I'd rather not think about him." He squeezed her hand. "Are you sure about this? I can't imagine what it must have been like, nearly being hauled off to the convent."

She shivered but nodded. "I'm sure."

"You should have told me about Burckhardt," he continued. "I would have—"

"That's exactly why I didn't tell you," she cut in. And why she wouldn't tell him about Burckhardt's latest attack. "You would have felt honor-bound to defend me. It would have looked suspicious if you had. Last thing we need is more suspicion." *Not to mention that Burckhardt is a hulking bully,* Francesca thought to herself. Phillip might have been hurt.

He frowned and let go of her hand and moved toward Achilles. "I enjoyed exercising Achilles for you. He made me feel less alone."

"Thank you for taking care of him." Francesca scratched Achilles behind the ear, and he nickered softly.

Phillip looked around. "Are we going to fence here?"

She shook her head. "It's a good meeting place, but it's too open and too close to home. I'm not taking any chances. I can't get you or anyone else in trouble again. We've got a bit further to go."

Phillip gave her a leg up into her side-saddle and swung up behind her.

As they followed the game trail, Francesca let herself ease back, little by little, until she leaned against his chest. She felt his body relax. He was so warm, so right. She knew it was scandalous, but she didn't care.

They reached the ruined stone barn far too soon. As Phillip dismounted and helped her down, he looked around and said, "This is perfect, but don't we need foils?"

"I've already hidden them here." She'd also rolled the stones that had tumbled from the old walls out of the way.

Francesca pushed back some of the white morning glories that covered one corner of the rubble and retrieved the practice blades. As she handed him one, Phillip said, "I still owe you that bout."

Excitement and emotion created a lump in Francesca's throat as she nodded. Her first real bout! She swallowed hard to stifle her anxiousness. She shouldn't do this. Fencing broke her vows, but she'd missed it so much. Holding the blade felt so natural, so much a part of who she was.

She hoped God could forgive her.

As she tucked her skirts up a couple inches and took her *en garde* position, their abbreviated bout sprang to mind and she giggled. "Remember the look on Signor Gallo's face when he walked in on us?"

Phillip chuckled. "Beyond price. Not to mention his hairy ankles." He stuck his neck out and pulled it back in a fair imitation of The Turtle. "What goes on here?"

"I'm going to beat you," she laughed. "That's what goes on here."

"Ha!" Phillip said with a grin as he took his position. "I'd like to see you try. Are you ready?"

"Yes, maestro."

They saluted each other, slashing their blades.

"Fence!"

Delicious fire ripped through her veins as she attacked in quick, controlled movements.

Phillip parried and backed away. His grin spread. "You'll have to do better than that."

She lunged again and again, attacking in high and lowline. She changed up the timing to keep him off guard. Phillip backed away, parrying and riposting. His blade flashed toward Francesca, and she responded.

The world fell away. Only they remained. In a fraction of a second her body reacted to the tiniest movement of his shoulder, the slightest shift of his weight, the tightening of his muscles that indicated an attack. Time and again her body knew where his blade would be and blocked quicker than her mind could react.

Fencing was a beautiful synchronicity of movement, give and take, as they moved first one way across the dirt floor then the other. It was like nothing Francesca had ever experienced. The movements were instinct, bone deep, but new and thrilling. For the first time, she felt completely free.

At the same time her mind floated above the bout, analyzing tactics, watching for weaknesses, assessing with a sharpness of focus, clarity, and elation she'd never felt before.

When Francesca landed the tip of her foil on his chest, Phillip called "Halt." They panted for breath.

Phillip shook his head slowly, mouth ajar. The look of respect on his face made Francesca's throat tighten. This was the first time someone had seen the real her, not the façade she wore daily, not the person they believed her to be. But her. Her fire, her passion, her skill. She blinked back tears.

"That was incredible," Phillip said.

Francesca nodded. "It was a hundred times better than I ever dreamed."

"You'd beat more than half the boys here, and that was your first bout!"

Francesca glowed.

He shook his head again. "If your father taught you, you'd be the best in the salle by now."

Francesca's breath caught. *If.* She dropped her blade and burst into tears. It was so unfair.

"I'm sorry." Phillip dropped his foil as well and moved toward her. "I meant it as a compliment. I didn't mean to upset you."

She stepped into him and pressed her face against his chest. He wrapped his arms around her. She felt ridiculous. *Stop it!* She told herself as she bit off her tears. *He'll think you're an idiot.* She pulled away.

"It's just, that's what I've always wanted," she said. "To be included. To be able to go to class with Papa, and you, and my brothers. To be able to fence and compete openly. But I'll always have to hide. I'll always have to be someone I'm not. I'll never be able to prove what I can do to anyone but you."

"You never have to pretend with me," he said.

She gave a weak smile, turned away, and wiped at her face. "I know it sounds silly, but, well, I always dreamed that someday, if maybe I were good enough, Papa would love me enough not to care what was proper. He wouldn't care what anyone said. He'd love me enough to teach me." She took a shaky breath.

She glanced at him, afraid he'd laugh at her.

His blue eyes shone. He gently turned her to face him. "That doesn't sound silly. I know how it feels to want a father's love," he said. "And I, for one, know who you are and what you can do, Francesca DiCesare. You're the most amazing woman I've ever met."

Suddenly she wasn't thinking of fencing, or Papa, or who knew what. Her whole world was the blue of his eyes, his dimples, and the sweet arch of his lips as he smiled. Yearning set her skin ablaze. She set her palm on his chest. His heart thundered under her hand. Her own pulse rushed to match it.

Eyes locked, he wrapped his hands around her waist. A shudder of anticipation swept through her. Her heart beat loud in her ears as she slid her arms around his neck. As he bent to kiss her, she lifted onto her toes to meet him.

His lips were soft and eager. Wherever his body touched hers ripples of flame spread outward. She pulled him harder against her to fan the flames. The passion overwhelmed and frightened her, which made it all the more intoxicating.

Phillip's hand slid up her back and into her hair at the nape of her neck. His lips traced the line of her jaw and throat. Then he whispered in her ear, "I love you, Francesca. Always."

CHAPTER 13
LEANDRO

The broken stone wall blocked out the warm afternoon sun and left Francesca and Phillip in cool, blue shade. Nonetheless, they were sweating.

"Halt!" called Phillip as he landed the tip of his practice foil on Francesca's ribcage. He grinned. "That's my point. Pay your forfeit."

"Gladly," she said with a smile, "since you paid so handsomely last time." She lowered her blade and stepped toward him. She put a hand around the back of his neck and drew his lips down to hers.

They'd been fencing at the barn whenever they could for the last two weeks. These days they barely got in a drill or two before they fell to fencing, and whoever lost the point had to give the other a kiss. Easily the most wonderful game ever.

Phillip wrapped his arms around her. Happiness bubbled through her as she nipped him playfully on the lower lip.

He lifted her up and spun her around. His flushed cheeks set off the blue of his eyes. Then he quirked his mouth. "Much as I hate to say it, we'd best get back." He gave her a kiss. "Next time, let's skip the fencing altogether."

She grinned. "You're not getting out of fencing with me that easily. And what about that duel you needed to fight so badly?" she teased.

The smile leached from his face, his jaw hardened, and his body tensed.

Francesca wished she could take her words back. "I'm sorry Phillip, I didn't mean..."

As he turned away, she followed him and put a hand on his arm. The sudden distance between them seemed unbearable.

"Phillip, talk to me. Who do you need to challenge?"

He ran a hand through his hair. "I've never told anyone."

Her heart ached for his pain. She entwined her fingers with his and led him over to some fallen stones to sit next to her. "You can tell me." She gave him a small smile and gestured toward the foils they'd dropped on the ground. "I'm good at keeping secrets."

He gave her a weak smile in return then lowered his eyes. She waited for him to begin.

"My father's a drunk, Francesca. And when he drinks, he gets vicious. Not that he's all that much better when he's sober." He took a breath. "He used to beat us, all of us—the whole household, really."

Francesca flushed with sudden fury at the man who would hurt her golden boy. Then she saw the long-held sorrow in Phillip and her fury drained away into sympathy.

He shifted uneasily. Francesca leaned against his shoulder and gripped his hand harder, willing his pain away. "I'm so sorry."

He glanced at her then looked off into the distance. "He beat my mother the worst." He shook his head. "As a child I remember the way she would wince when I tried to hug her. Once he broke her arm."

"Is she…"

"She died ten years ago from a fall from a balcony. I was eight at the time. But as I got older, I began to think more about that fall."

Francesca gasped. "My God, Phillip. You don't think…"

His jaw muscles tensed under the skin. "He's a monster, Francesca. He drove her to it. She couldn't take it anymore. He killed her."

Francesca shook her head, confused. "I don't understand."

"I was only a child, but I saw what she went through. It was the only way she could get away from him."

"Are you saying he pushed her?" She couldn't imagine the kind of pain he must feel.

"I think she threw herself off, but he might as well have done it."

He eased away and looked her in the eye. His voice was hard, almost brutal. "I need to confront him. I need to make him pay. I intend to challenge him. I owe my mother that. She was the only good thing about my childhood."

She tried to soothe him. "But you don't know for sure. Maybe she tripped. People fall all the time. It was just an accident. Everything will be all right."

"Maybe," Phillip said. "But when he's sober, my father is wicked fast with a blade. I need to be ready."

"You can't challenge your own father," she said. "It's just too horrible. It's not—"

"Honorable?" Phillip rose and paced. His eyes glistened with unshed tears. "Don't you think I've thought about this? How can I not? How will my mother ever have justice? How will I, if I don't see it through?"

Francesca went to him and wrapped him in her arms. "I was going to say, 'It's not fair.' You shouldn't have to deal with this on your own. I'm sorry that you have to go through this."

He softened and put his arms around her.

"But you were only a child," she said. "Maybe it was just a horrible, tragic accident."

"Maybe," he said. He hugged her to him fiercely. She felt a tear land on top of her head.

"Thank you," he said. "It feels good to have someone to talk to."

She looked up into his eyes as he dashed away a tear. "You can tell me anything. You already know my biggest secret."

He smiled. "I think I am your biggest secret."

She chuckled. "Yes, you are."

When he bent and kissed her, she melted against him, hoping to take some of his pain and worry onto her own shoulders.

"I love you, Francesca," he said. "And anyway, England is a long way from here." He took a deep breath. "I suppose we had better get back."

They collected their foils, wrapped them in oiled canvas and slipped them into their hiding spot behind the pile of blossom-strewn rubble.

They were quiet as they rode Achilles back to the climbing tree. Francesca felt the weight of Phillip's words. The quest that had seemed so romantic when he first mentioned it months ago now filled her with dread.

Phillip swept Francesca's hair out of the way and kissed her neck. "I'm sorry for burdening you with my problems."

"No! Oh no." She leaned into him and put her hand over his. "I'm glad you told me. It's, well, these have been the happiest two weeks of my life. And now, the future is … I feel like this is too good to last."

"I'm not going anywhere. I promise," he said. "We were meant to be together. I know it."

"But that isn't enough, is it?" She thought of Catalina and Sebi. "No matter what kind of a man your father is, you're still a nobleman, and I'm, I'm just the maestro's daughter."

They'd arrived at the climbing tree and Phillip swung off Achilles's back. "You're not 'just' anything. You're the love of my life. Let me worry about the future." He smiled. "You just focus on your point control. You were dropping your tip again today. Keep your blade up and you might just beat me next time."

Phillip bowed deeply with a theatrical sweep of his arm. "My lady," he said, then disappeared into the brush.

Francesca mused as she collected Mateo and Reginia and rode toward the salle. She couldn't imagine the horror of growing up in such an abusive household. And his poor mother. It couldn't be true.

And dear Catalina about to be married off to God-knows-who. What if her husband … Francesca shivered. She couldn't bear the thought.

Helplessness gnawed at her. She had run out of ideas on how to save Catalina. And spending time with Phillip only made her want more: more time with him, more closeness, more him. Now she had to go back and pretend she had never seen or spoken to him. Life seemed so wrong and she didn't know how to fix any of it.

When Francesca and Mateo cantered around the side of the stable, Cassio and the grooms were staring down the road and students running back and forth across the courtyard calling to each other.

"What's going on?" Francesca asked Cassio in alarm.

Cassio grinned and pointed into the distance to a rider on a bay horse followed by a cart.

"Papa!" Francesca cried, elated. She clapped her heel against Achilles' side and bolted down the road to welcome him home.

"Cesca, my dear!" Papa called out as she approached. "How lovely you look. A woman grown. If your dark hair had more than just that touch of red, you'd be the very image of your mother."

"I'm so happy you're home!" Francesca slid from the saddle before Achilles had come to a complete stop. "I missed you so."

"And I you." He reined in and swung out of his saddle. He gave her a warm bear-hug and she squeezed him tight, safe and happy in his arms.

She took his hand, and they walked a ways, leading their horses.

An olive-green, heavily laden cart pulled by two weary horses creaked and thumped along the rutted road a dozen paces behind them.

A layer of tan road dust covered Papa's hair, skin, and riding jacket. He was wan, thinner than when he'd left, his cheekbones and scars more prominent, though his back was as straight and his gray eyes as bright as ever.

"How was your journey, Papa?"

"Long," he said, "though I'm home earlier than I had planned." He shook his head. "And not as fruitful as I had hoped. I missed Billy entirely. He's off to the English colonies with his new bride. It's a risky affair at best. Now we must trust to fate that he'll be well."

"I'm sorry to hear it Papa," she said, not caring in the least about some man she'd never met. "You look tired."

"Never go to sea if you can help it, my dear. The deck heaves and bucks so violently under your feet, and your stomach with it. There's no sleep to be had. But a few nights in my own bed and I'll be my old self, no doubt."

Francesca wondered if she'd dislike the sea as much as Papa. In all the books she read it sounded wonderful, an endless adventure full of possibility and freedom, where one never knew what might happen just over the horizon.

They remounted their horses and continued on.

"What news here?" asked Papa.

Francesca's mind went immediately to Maestro Ferro and Signora Bianchi escorting her to the carriage to take her to the convent. She suppressed a shiver. Papa would likely be furious with her and she didn't want to spoil his homecoming. She shrugged, glanced over her shoulder at the dusty cart that followed them, nodded briefly at the driver who tipped his dusty hat, and said, "What's in the wagon, Papa?"

"Ah, yes," some new mannequins, practice foils, and fencing jackets for the salle. Some books, and maybe," he said with a wink, "some gifts for you and your brothers. Though I think those can wait until after dinner."

His voice dropped a note. "But you've changed the subject."

"Well," Francesca said. "Leandro broke a blade and stabbed Sebi in the leg, and Signor Gallo had to have a tooth knocked out."

The maestro nodded. "Yes, but you've neglected a few items. I received a letter from Signora Bianchi just as I was leaving England."

Francesca's stomach tightened and she dropped her eyes. So much for not ruining his homecoming, but Papa always took the bull by the horns.

He glanced back at the driver on the cart out of earshot behind them. His face darkened and his voice grew sharp. "Lord Ernst will leave the salle as soon as can be arranged. And I'll inform Maestro Ferro that in the future he'd best err on the side of protecting my family rather than protecting the reputation of the salle."

He softened, reached over, and squeezed her hand. "I'm glad that you did not suffer worse at Lord Ernst's hands."

A weight lifted from her shoulders. She hadn't realized how much Burckhardt's hulking presence and watchful eyes had plagued her. She gave Papa a half smile, then waited for what she knew would come next.

"As for your fencing alone with Lord Worthington," continued Papa. "I'm angry and disappointed that you would go against my wishes."

He studied her for a moment and she dropped her eyes.

"I only wanted to learn to defend myself," she said, sticking to the story she'd told the signora.

He watched her face carefully as he said, a little less sternly, "Lord Worthington is a very handsome young man."

Francesca felt a blush. Although Papa hadn't actually asked a question, she knew what he was implying. She considered her answer carefully.

"I'd be lying if I said I hadn't noticed," she said. "But honestly Papa, it was the fencing I was interested in."

Papa sighed and ran a hand through the graying hair at his temples. "To be honest, I'm not sure which answer would be more alarming."

Francesca hung her head. They rode on silently for a moment, then Papa reined in his horse. When she stopped beside him, he turned to her.

"As you've already been copiously punished by our good signora, I'll say no more, except this: the rules I set down are for your own good. You are young and passionate and have little experience with the wider world. I only wish to protect you. Even if that means protecting you from yourself."

Francesca bristled as he ran a hand down his face.

"I don't want you to go near a sword," he said.

"Yes, Papa," she replied out of habit, putting on her dutiful face to hide her frustration.

Why does everyone think they need to protect me? I'm a grown woman. I can take care of myself.

It wasn't like she wanted to use sharps or anything. Why couldn't she use practice blades? Perhaps a blade broke now and then and someone was injured like Sebi had been, but no one had ever been killed, and the danger was part of the fun.

Behind her frustration lurked guilt. What would Papa do if he knew she was still fencing with Phillip, and kissing him as well? He'd send Phillip away for starters. He might even order her to Colleviti for her own protection. Still, despite the risk, she knew she wouldn't quit.

As they neared the stables, students and staff poured out the main gates all talking at once. They surrounded Papa and welcomed him home. Francesca left him to the crowd and took Achilles to the stable.

As she unbridled Achilles, Phillip ducked into the stable.

Francesca's heart sped and she glanced around to make sure they were alone. "You shouldn't be here. They mustn't see us together."

"I had to see you," Phillip said with a smile. "I'm so happy that your father has returned. I've something important to ask him."

She tilted her head, confused. Then her eyes widened and she gasped. "You mean..." Could he mean he wanted to ask for her hand? Was it possible? Would their parents allow it? His blood was blue and hers was not. It simply was not done.

"I do." He took her face in his hands, kissed her, then hurried toward the stable door. "Expect good news when we meet tomorrow."

"Wait!"

He was gone. She stared after him wanting to dash into the courtyard and stop him, talk to him, but she couldn't be seen with him. She wanted to tell him not to say anything, that what they had was too precious to risk. If Papa said no, then everything would be lost.

Doubt and hope warred in her chest. He seemed so confident. Francesca had heard stories of people marrying into the noble classes. The romantic stories that Catalina loved were full of such things. Francesca had always doubted they were true, but it wasn't impossible, was it?

After what Phillip had told her about his father, she didn't know what to think. Would such a man care about the differences between them? Would he think her too far beneath Phillip? Phillip certainly seemed less haughty and superior than most of the nobles she'd met.

Papa had no reason to say no. Noble relations could help his business.

Marriage! In the past the idea had horrified her, but how wonderful it would be to marry Phillip. She'd finally be able to fence whenever and wherever she liked without hiding!

Signora Bianchi was wrong; she could have love and fencing too. Perhaps they could have adventure as well. Maybe they could even explore the New World together. What an exquisite life they would have! Of course, there would be children, but even that didn't seem so terrible if she was with Phillip.

She hid her excitement as Cassio and the grooms returned with Papa's bay and she brushed Achilles down.

She wanted to run out and tell Catalina, but then, Catalina was so anxious and unhappy. It seemed cruel to tell her the wonderful news.

Where was Catalina anyway? Francesca hadn't seen her among the group that welcomed Papa. Why hadn't she been at the stable as usual when Francesca arrived? Catalina was still under orders not to leave Francesca's side since no one trusted Burckhardt, though she felt reasonably safe.

Worried, she put away the curry brush and hurried into the salle to find Catalina.

The courtyard had emptied except for servants who unloaded the cart that had accompanied Papa home and a few straggling students. Dinner time was near, so Francesca headed upstairs. She checked Catalina's room before she stopped in her own room to change out of her riding habit, but Catalina wasn't there.

As she went downstairs, she heard the tinkling crash of broken glass from down the hall. She hurried to the doorway of the family dining room.

The table was set, yellow candlelight glinting off their best glassware and silver in celebration of Papa's homecoming. Beyond it, Catalina stood by the red marble fireplace. Her hands covered her face, and she was crying. A dark splash of water and a pile of broken glass against the wall showed where a pitcher had been hurled against the tapestry. Sebi paced, his body tense, his face dark, and a piece of paper clutched in his hand.

Catalina wiped at her tears.

Francesca felt heavy with dread as she went to Catalina and hugged her.

"What is it?" asked Francesca.

"Leandro!" Sebi said, his voice thick and harsh. He crushed the paper in his hands.

"What about him?" Francesca felt sick to her stomach.

Catalina gave a hiccupping cry, broke away, and ran from the room.

Sebi stopped pacing. The anger ebbed out of him and he hung his head. "She's going to marry him."

"No, oh no!" Francesca said. She rushed after Catalina.

On the way out of the dining room she nearly plowed into Papa and Antonio.

Papa, washed and in fresh clothes, said, "What is this? What happened? Catalina just ran by in tears."

Francesca steadied her voice. "Catalina is to be married to Leandro."

"Bollocks," Antonio said.

Papa's face softened. "Go on then." He hitched his head in the direction of the stairs. "See to her. We'll see to Sebi."

As Francesca ran up the stairs, her sorrow for Catalina turned into anger at Catalina's parents. How could they so blatantly ignore Catalina's wishes! It was not as if Leandro's family had better blood or more wealth than the DiCesares. Leandro's father was a public official, no more. The decision made no sense.

She knocked softly on Catalina's door. Catalina opened it and drew her into a hug. Her sobbing intensified as they sank down onto the edge of the bed. Francesca held her and cried, too. She wished she knew what to say to comfort her friend. All she could think of were useless platitudes. Everything would not be all right, not ever again.

Eventually Catalina quieted. She pulled a handkerchief from her pocket and wiped her eyes and nose.

"Maybe, well, maybe we can convince them to change their minds," Francesca finally said. "It's not as if Leandro is a better catch than Sebi."

Catalina went to the window and stared out. She shook her head. "My father won't change his mind. This is a business decision."

"How is Leandro supposed to help your father's business?" Francesca said, confused.

"Business is suffering because we have fewer and fewer places to sell our silks. France no longer allows importers to sell silk there, and England has begun their own silk production."

"I remember, but what does that have to do with Leandro?" Francesca said.

"His father is vice-governor of Cartagena. With this alliance Father can sell his silks all over the New World, the Caribbean, and possibly Spain as well. Those are enormous silk markets." Catalina took a deep breath.

"Father won't let that go just because…" Her voice caught, her eyes filling with longing and tears. "Just because I'm in love."

A weight dropped through Francesca's stomach. Catalina's marriage to Leandro was worth a literal fortune to her father. How could Sebi possibly compete with that?

Francesca's thoughts went to Phillip and a knot formed in her belly. Would his father think her worth enough to marry his son?

"When is the wedding?" asked Francesca, defeated.

Catalina wiped her eyes again. "I don't know exactly, but we leave for Cartagena in a week."

"Cartagena!"

Catalina nodded and gasped through her tears, "That's where we'll be living."

"Oh, Catalina, I'm so sorry." Francesca went to her and hugged her again. *The New World.* Life was so unfair. Francesca would love to see the wonders of the Spanish colonies, the mighty Amazon River, the volcanos, and the hills of El Dorado, but she knew that was the last thing in the world Catalina wanted. Catalina had no interest in adventure. She wanted home and family. But she might never see her family again, and Francesca might never see her again. She might as well be on the moon as across the Atlantic Ocean.

Francesca's heart broke for Catalina and Sebi. She tried desperately to come up with some way to save them. She felt guilty that despite her sadness, she still couldn't help thinking of Phillip asking Papa for her hand.

Emotions played across Catalina's face. Francesca could only imagine how frightened she must be considering an uncertain future with a man she barely knew so far from home.

Francesca wished she could ask Nana's advice. Nana would know what to do. She couldn't take away Catalina's pain or change her father's mind—not with so much at stake. Even if she did send a letter to Leandro's father and somehow convince him to stop the wedding, Catalina and Leandro would be gone before the letter even arrived, and then it would most likely be too late.

The only one she could actually speak to was Leandro. *What if Leandro refused to marry Catalina?* Would his parents force him, or would they find him another bride? Would Catalina's parents then consider Sebi as an alternative? *Could I convince Leandro not to marry Catalina? And if so, how?*

CHAPTER 14
NOT EVIL

Achilles pawed a patch of wispy grass beneath the lightning-scarred oak, as though he sensed Francesca's agitation. She sat on the fallen branch and picked at the bark. She would have paced, but her legs felt too weak.

Dark clouds hung purple and ominous overhead, nearly scraping the top of the tree as she waited for Phillip to appear at their usual time. She vacillated between wild hope and dread. She refused to take the clouds as a bad omen. There was enough sadness already at the salle, there had to be some good news. Papa just had to say yes to Phillip's proposal.

The underbrush off to her left rustled. Francesca's breath caught as she turned to look.

Phillip's face was hard and tight.

Her breath hissed out and she trembled as she rose to meet him. He folded her in his arms.

She held on to him, her cheek against his shoulder, listening to the beating of his heart.

Finally she said, "Papa said no." She looked up at him.

He shook his head.

Confused, she pulled away. "Then, what happened?"

Phillip ran a hand over his face. He turned away and paced through the leaflitter at the base of the climbing tree. The rising wind picked up the leaves and whirled them around the clearing.

"I had just gotten up the nerve to speak to your father when he found me. He had a letter for me." His voice turned into a snarl. "Christ, Francesca, my father…" He fell silent.

Alarm spiraled through her. "What about him? Has something happened to him?"

"It's not that."

"Then, what is it?"

He paced faster, kicking up the dead leaves, and then stopped suddenly and turned to her. "She's an old lady," he said bitterly. "She's thirty-five if she's a day, and so sickly it's a miracle she's outlasted two husbands."

"Who is?" Fear bunched in her stomach. "Phillip, what's happened?"

"My father has already chosen a wife for me."

"He … oh! But he can't!" Emptiness swallowed her.

"The Countess Wentworth," Phillip said through gritted teeth.

"A contessa!" Francesca put a hand to her mouth. Phillip would be marrying far above a lordship—instead of marrying down to Francesca's level. She was a nobody, just the maestro's daughter.

"How? Why would she—"

He shrugged. "I don't know. All I know is that I'm ordered to leave for England as soon as can be arranged."

The air left her lungs and she couldn't breathe. She was choking, drowning in a dark room. She couldn't lose him too, her charming, handsome Phillip. How was she to live without being able to see him, touch him, and hear his voice? He was the only one who knew the real her, who let her be herself. Without him and Catalina she'd have nothing. She'd be all alone.

"She's rich as Midas," Phillip said. "That's why my father wants me to marry her, so he can get his hands on her money."

Panic set in. She bent over, as her vision narrowed. The sound of a hawk crying in a nearby tree was drowned by a hissing in her ears. How could she go back to the nothingness she had lived in for months?

Phillip helped her sit on the fallen branch. He took her face in both his hands. His eyes, locked to hers, were angry. "I won't do it. He can damn well marry her himself."

His shoulders squared and a determined smile lit his face. "I want to marry *you*, Francesca. I want to be your husband." Suddenly his face was shy, vulnerable, "If you'll have me."

"Oh, Phillip," she cried, wracked by sorrow. "Of course I would. I love you so much. I wish..." She wiped at her tears. How could anyone as perfect as Phillip love her? She had found him, the one man in all the world who could love her, and then to have him taken away. "I wish we could be together."

He smiled, cupped her face in his hands, and gently wiped away her tears with his thumbs. He kissed her tenderly. "We can. All we have to do is elope."

Francesca's eyes widened. A wild, reckless hope ignited in her. She wouldn't be alone, and she'd be free to be herself, always. She'd never have to pretend or hide again.

It was a crazy, dangerous idea.

How exciting!

Her only knowledge of such things came from Catalina's talk of the romantic novels she read. Her mind conjured images of mad, romantic rushes together on horseback across verdant fields chased by half-seen figures, stolen moments hidden away in exotic places, couples pledging their undying love. Maybe that was all fantasy, but Catalina was already fated to go to the new world. Perhaps they could sneak off to Cartagena with her. A shiver ran through her body. She wanted to shout YES, but she hesitated.

Papa will be hurt.

She hated the idea of causing him pain. He would miss her, and she'd miss him. Could he ever forgive her for the embarrassment it would cause him, the dishonor? He might never speak to her again. Could she live with that?

Phillip's father might disown him.

She thought about her discussion with Catalina about money, about the people living on the street in Casina. She wondered for the first time who they were and what they did before they were forced onto the street.

"How would we manage?" she asked in a small voice.

This seemed like the time for boldness and grand gestures, not mundane concerns about money, but she was scared. If they did this, they would be on their own, they couldn't count on help from anyone.

"I have some money of my own," Phillip said. "It will last until I can find employment. My Italian might not be great, but I'm good with numbers. And if that fails, well, I have a strong back."

Francesca's breath caught. Phillip was willing to give up everything to be with her. "But your inheritance, your title!"

He looked away. "I won't be like him—obsessed with money," he said. "My father is a greedy bastard. What money he has, he's swindled from nearly everyone he knows, and ruined our reputation in the process. That's why he's arranged this marriage, I'm sure. Another swindle."

He turned back to her, his blue eyes bright. "But I don't give a whit for any inheritance if I can be with you."

Reservations and fears melted in the aqua certainty in his eyes that left no room for doubt. She and Phillip were smart, and they were strong. As long as they had each other, they'd find a way to be happy no matter the circumstances. She was sure of it.

"Of course I'll run away with you."

Phillip's face glowed and his shoulders relaxed. He crushed her tight against his chest. "My God, Francesca, you're wonderful. Tonight. Meet me in the stable at midnight."

She snuggled into his arms, the place where she was home, safe, and loved. He was all she wanted, whatever might happen. Nothing else mattered. When he bent to kiss her, the tenderness and promise in his touch brought tears of happiness to her eyes.

Now that they had decided, a surge of frantic energy gripped Francesca. She rose and headed toward Achilles, but Phillip caught her wrist. "Wait," he said. "If you go back too early they might get suspicious."

"But there's so much to do. I have to pack. And Catalina—"

"You can't tell her, Francesca. You can't tell anyone."

She paused. How could she *not* tell Catalina?

"But she could help us."

"We can't take the risk. She may not understand. She might tell."

"I'm sure she…" Francesca trailed off. Would Catalina understand? Catalina was willing to give up her own happiness for her family, always believing in duty first. Francesca could almost hear Catalina say she was ruining her life. Catalina wouldn't understand that this was the only way and would try to talk her out of it. If that failed, would she tell Sebi? Would he try to stop them? Phillip was right. They couldn't take the chance.

But how could she leave her best friend without a word just a week before she was sent to the New World to marry a man she barely knew? How could Catalina ever forgive her?

But ...

What if she could make sure Catalina didn't have to go? What if she could arrange for Catalina to marry Sebi?

Sebi might not have ties to Spain, but he could sell silks, she was sure of it. Enzo was already working to help the family business. Why did they need Catalina to give up her home, her future, and the man she loved?

I can do this.

She would save Catalina so that she could leave with a clear conscience. Somehow. That would be her farewell gift to Catalina. Francesca had to talk to Leandro before she and Phillip left. She had to convince him not to marry Catalina.

She nodded to Phillip. "I won't tell a soul, but there is something I need to do before we go. If I arrive back at the usual time, Catalina will be waiting for me and I won't have the chance. I need to get back early."

"Very well." Phillip drew her back into his arms. "But not *too* early," he breathed. He kissed her with a passion that sent fire rippling along her skin. She answered his passion with her own. Her tongue flicked against his lips, exploring. Phillip gasped as she wrapped her fingers in his golden hair, her lips tracing his jawline.

"Oh, God." He shuddered and eased himself away from her. "Tonight. After we're married."

———

Francesca was so distracted on the way back to the salle, she nearly forgot to collect Mateo and Reginia. Her mind buzzed with half-formed plans and anticipation as she rode through the whipping wind full of the smell of rain. She needed to focus, to marshal her arguments for Leandro.

Unfortunately, those arguments were few. How was she supposed to convince him not to marry someone as smart, kind, and beautiful as Catalina? Only two arguments came to mind.

First, Leandro's father was vice-governor of Cartagena. That meant that someday soon he might be made governor, and with that appointment usually came lands and title. Once Leandro had a title, he'd have his choice of noble women with more property and fortune than Catalina.

That argument depended on a lot of circumstances and required a certain amount of greed on Leandro's part. She didn't know him well, but he'd been at the salle for nearly four years, and she'd never seen any signs of avarice or ambition. And like most of the young men at the salle, she had seen his eyes follow Catalina on occasion.

Her second argument was to tell Leandro that Catalina was in love with Sebi. She would have to be careful not to cast any hint of impropriety, or Catalina's reputation could be ruined. Such a strategy might backfire. While Francesca had never known Leandro to be greedy, he was supremely competitive, especially with Sebi, who was the only student among his peers more skilled than him. Leandro might be thrilled to beat Sebi out of a bride. If only it were a fair fight.

A fair fight!

She reined Achilles in, and Mateo and Regina passed by, heading for the stable.

That was it! Sebi could challenge Leandro for Catalina's hand. Sebi would win, she was sure. Sebi had more incentive, and he was the better fencer, perhaps not by much, but better. Catalina wouldn't like being treated like a prize. Francesca didn't like the thought either, but it beat the alternative.

She pictured Sebi and Leandro on the dueling grounds, under the massive elm as Catalina watched with her hands pressed nervously to her mouth. She imagined the point of Sebi's practice blade landing a perfect touch on Leandro's chest, and the officiant shouting, "Point and match, Sebastian!" She could almost see the joy on Sebi's and Catalina's faces as they turned toward each other and Leandro dropped his head in defeat.

Having watched Leandro bout for years, she was certain she could make it happen. His weaknesses were so obvious—she'd seen them over and over, and she could advise Sebi just as she had Phillip. She would make sure Sebi won.

She slapped the reins against Achilles' neck and urged him into a gallop, passing Mateo.

"What's the hurry?" called Mateo.

"I'm going to save Catalina!"

When she reached the stable, she handed Achilles off to Cassio and hurried toward the salle. Burckhardt glared at her from across the courtyard, but she didn't care. By Papa's orders, he would leave tomorrow afternoon on a coach from Cascina to the Port of Livorno, and then off to whatever rock he'd crawled out from under.

As she approached the double doors, she wondered for a moment how to find Sebi, but that was obvious. He'd be with Catalina if he could. This time of day Catalina was likely in the sewing room with Signora Bianchi. The signora would probably not allow Sebi to accompany Catalina after the announcement of her wedding, but Sebi would be close by, hoping to see her when she was done with her chores.

Sure enough, she spotted him upstairs in the family sitting room, next to the sewing room. The door between the two rooms was open and Francesca saw her governess in the room beyond, head bent over her embroidery.

Sebi sat five paces away from Francesca. He pretended to read a book, but his leg bounced nervously, he never turned the page, and he glanced regularly toward the sewing room. Francesca couldn't see his expression, but his shoulders were slumped and his fingers, on the leather arms of his chair, picked at the fabric.

She didn't dare enter the sitting room. If the signora saw her, she'd be ordered into the sewing room to work on her own embroidery, and she needed to speak with Sebi alone.

She waved at him from the doorway, but he never looked around at her. She searched her skirt pocket and found an old, dented pewter thimble. Taking careful aim, she threw it at him. The thimble bounced off his shoulder and Sebi turned. Francesca put one finger to her lips and beckoned him with the other hand.

Sebastian glanced again toward the sewing room, set the book aside, and rose. He hurried toward her and whispered, "What are you up to now?"

She hushed him, took his arm, and drew him around the corner into their old nursery and playroom.

The afternoon sun streamed through the window lighting up the threadbare rug and the bookcase full of forgotten toys as she closed the door behind them.

Francesca faced Sebi, noting the circles under his eyes and the paleness of his skin around a day's growth of patchy beard. His clothes looked rumpled and unkempt.

"I've done it," she said. "I figured out how you can marry Catalina."

"What are you talking about?" Anger clouded his face and red patches showed on his cheeks. "It's already been decided. She's to marry Leandro." He ground out Leandro's name between his teeth.

"Not if Leandro refuses to marry her," she said.

"And why would he do that?" Sebi said, growing more agitated.

"Because honor demanded it!"

Sebi ran a hand through his unruly auburn curls. "Just tell me what the blazes you're talking about!"

"Hush!" said Francesca glancing nervously at the door. "I'm talking about you challenging Leandro to a duel for Catalina's hand."

He shook his head. "Don't you think I've thought of that? He'd never agree. Why should he? He's already got the prize."

"He can hardly refuse a challenge," she said. "That would be dishonorable. Especially if you threaten to tell everyone he's a coward if he doesn't accept. He wouldn't want to appear craven in front of his bride to be." She shrugged. "Besides, you could tell him it's for his peace of mind. If he doesn't win her, for the rest of their life together he'll wonder if Catalina is thinking about you instead of him."

Sebi stared at her for a moment, then shook his head. "You are an evil little minx, aren't you?"

She frowned. "Not evil, determined. I'm not going to let Catalina's father break up our family and send her off to kingdom come just to line his own pockets."

Sebi's face went still. His eyes narrowed and he stared, unseeing, at the bookcase, as if picturing something in his mind. Then his hand went to his thigh, to the spot where Leandro had accidentally stabbed him. "It might work," he said. "If I get him angry enough, he might agree."

"I know he will." She nodded. "He's arrogant. He won't pass up a chance to rub your face in his victory."

Sebi straightened his shoulders and his jaws tightened. "I'll challenge him, God help me. There's nothing left for me without Catalina."

"You'll win. I know you will. You're better than he is."

Sebastian puffed out his cheeks.

"You are," she said. "Besides, Leandro always signals his attacks. Whenever he's about to lunge, he drops his right shoulder an inch or two. When he does, retreat, then hit him on the counterattack. He never double lunges."

Sebi raised his eyebrows but didn't comment. He put a hand on her shoulder and gave a quick squeeze. "Wish me luck." Then he was gone.

CHAPTER 15
BURCKHARDT'S FAULT

As she hurried to her room, Francesca buzzed with excitement. Now that Catalina would soon to be rescued, she could concentrate on her own future with Phillip.

Pulling an old leather portmanteau from her armoire, she set it on her bed. The cracked ox hide smelled of leather, dust, and adventure.

She put in what little money she had: a half-dozen liras, and a handful of soldi—enough to feed her and Phillip for a few weeks if they were careful.

Then she took her mother-of-pearl jewelry box from her shelf and opened it, scanning the glistening contents. Most was costume jewelry—enameled combs, copper or bronze brooches, colorful pins Papa had brought back from his trips as souvenirs that Francesca kept for the memories—but some had been her mother's and Nana's.

Francesca put on the silver locket that held an auburn curl of her mother's hair that Papa had given her on her sixth birthday. She took out a pearl necklace and a ruby ring that had belonged to her mother and laid them on the bed. Next to them she placed a sapphire brooch and matching earrings that had belonged to Nana. All but the ring she wrapped carefully and set in the bag, glad to think that something of her mother and Nana would be going with her. The ring she slipped on her finger.

Next, she sorted through her clothing. As she worked, she wondered where she and Phillip would go. Cascina, an hour away on horseback, was the nearest town, but they might be better off going on to Livorno. That would mean another hour of travel, but Livorno was a much larger city, and there was less chance she would be recognized. Livorno was also a port if they decided to go to sea. *To sea! How exciting that would be.*

She was sure that once the shock and anger of their elopement wore off, Papa would forgive them. After all, he had often told her and her brothers how he had married their mother for love, not alliance or money as most did. He could hardly fault her for doing the same. Perhaps they could even come back here, eventually—after they'd had their fill of adventure. And if her plan worked and Catalina was free to marry Sebi, what a wonderful time they would all have together.

Catalina's soft knock on the door snapped her out of her thoughts. She set the bag on the floor and shoved it under her bed with her foot.

When she opened the door, Catalina's eyes and nose were red, as if she'd been crying recently, but her eyebrows and lips were pinched in a frown of annoyance.

"I waited for you at the stable," Catalina said.

"I'm so sorry!" Francesca had forgotten that Catalina would meet her after her ride. "I returned a little early." She drew Catalina into the room. "I came up to change and lost track of time. Please don't be cross with me."

"Oh, it's all right." Catalina sank down onto the bed.

This would be their last few hours together—at least until Papa forgave her. Tears gathered in Francesca's eyes, and she turned away so Catalina wouldn't see. The ache of missing her friend had already begun. She couldn't imagine life without her.

"How was your ... ride?" Catalina teased.

Francesca quickly blinked away her tears and smiled. She could barely keep her secrets from bursting from her lips, but Catalina wouldn't understand.

"Wonderful," she replied sitting next to Catalina. "I wish I could tell you how wonderful."

Catalina grinned back, though her smile was tinged with sadness.

She is so amazing, thought Francesca. *How can she be happy for me, when she's so sad for herself and Sebi?*

Francesca looked around the bedroom she would never sleep in again. She wanted to give Catalina something to remember her by, something precious, just in case things went badly and Papa refused to forgive them.

Then there was a chance her plan for Sebi and Leandro wouldn't work. In which case, they might never see each other again.

She blinked back tears as she slid the ruby ring from her finger and turned to Catalina. "You're my best friend in the whole world, Catalina. I'd like you to have this."

Catalina's dark eyes widened in surprise. "But that was your mother's!"

"It's yours now."

Catalina shook her head. "I couldn't, Franny. It means so much to you."

"Please," Francesca insisted. "I want you to remember me when you wear it."

"Why don't you think about it? There's plenty of time."

Francesca took Catalina's hand and placed the ring in it. "No, I want you to have it now, in case, well, things might get busy later."

Catalina fingered the ring and slipped it on. "It's beautiful. But I could never forget you, Franny. These years with you have meant so much." Her eyes filled with tears. "Oh Franny, I'm frightened! I know it's for the best, but everything will be so different, and I'll be so far away. I wish I could stay here with you and Sebi." Her face crumbled and she began to cry.

Francesca hugged her, then wiped the tears from Catalina's cheeks. "It's all right, Catalina. Don't cry." She hesitated, then added. "You won't have to go anywhere. I've fixed it."

Catalina looked at her sharply. "What do you mean you've fixed it? It's already been decided. There's nothing you can do."

Francesca was a little hurt by the dismissal in Catalina's voice. "Well, I, I convinced Sebi to fight for you."

"Fight for me? Don't be—" She stopped, and her face went pale. Catalina grabbed Francesca's upper arms and her fingers dug in. "What do you mean?"

"He's going to challenge Leandro for your hand."

"My God, Francesca, what have you done?"

"What's wrong?" Francesca asked. "I thought you'd be happy. Sebi is better than Leandro. I know he'll win."

"He could be killed!" Catalina rose from the bed.

"The chances of another blade breaking are—"

"On the way back from the stable I saw Burckhardt." Her voice rose nearly to hysteria. "He was carrying sharps!"

A sink hole opened in the bottom of Francesca's stomach.

"They wouldn't!" Francesca rushed to the window. "Sharps are against the rules."

Wind whipped the giant elm that towered over the dueling grounds beyond the stone wall. She spotted a mob in shirtsleeves and caught the flash of blades beneath the tree. She couldn't tell if they were sharps or practice blades, but the duel had already begun.

"Oh God!"

She turned toward Catalina who was already headed for the door.

"We have to stop them," Catalina said as they rushed down the stairs.

Francesca, lifting her skirts and taking the steps two and three at a time, quickly outpaced Catalina. She sprinted through the main hall with The Turtle, off to her right, commanding her not to run. As she crossed the courtyard, two or three boys hurried in the same direction, and she heard shouts from beyond the stone wall.

Dusk was falling when Francesca flew around the corner of the stable. Most of the students had gathered in the twilight under the massive elm. Francesca could see nothing but backs, but she heard blades clank and hiss like angry metallic snakes. The crowd seemed strangely eager, twitchy, full of restless energy.

Francesca and Catalina pushed their way through the crowd using their elbows.

"Thank God!" Catalina breathed, when they reached the front.

Sebi and Leandro held practice blades, not sharps, and Francesca's stomach unclenched a bit, but there was something seriously wrong. These were not the fencers she knew.

It had always been a pleasure to watch Sebi and Leandro bout, a ballet of movement, a display of technique. They were calm, dispassionate, and cerebral, every movement considered and weighed.

Now their faces were red masks of hatred, their actions aggressive and wild. Francesca realized with shock, this was not a fencing match, but a dog fight, and the crowd of boys knew it and urged them on, feeding the rage. That was the twitchiness and anticipation she had felt from the crowd; they were hoping for spilled blood, encouraging it. She shook her head. Sebi needed calm and focus now more than ever. Why had he let Leandro take that from him?

The officiant was a lanky French boy, Henri, who Francesca barely knew but who had a reputation for fairness. He moved with Sebi and

Leandro as he watched their actions to make sure no one cheated. The three of them circled and moved back and forth together inside the uneven ring of the crowd. Sebi and Leandro must each have two "seconds" to make sure the duel was properly carried out, but who they were among the crowd, she couldn't tell.

Francesca yelled for Henri to stop the duel, but her voice was swallowed up in the noise of the crowd.

Leandro and Sebi paused in their circling, with Leandro's back to Francesca. He lunged. Francesca couldn't see the action through Leandro, but there was a shout from Sebi, echoed by the crowd. Leandro backed away and to the left. A red welt now lined Sebi's cheekbone, and his eyes burned with fury.

Catalina took a sharp breath.

Francesca tensed. That had been perilously close to Sebi's eye. They were trying to seriously hurt each other. She didn't understand. All Sebi had to do was win. No one needed to get hurt.

Sebi attacked recklessly, his point wide, his body off balance. His blade came up far short. He attacked again, without first finding his footing and gauging his opponent.

How could his emotions have undone Papa's training so quickly? *Sebi, calm down,* Francesca thought. *Control! You have to win this!* He was too wild, too desperate. It made him an easy target.

They circled again. Now Sebi's back was to the girls. Francesca saw Leandro drop his shoulder an inch. *Sebi, back off! Let him attack. Hit him on the counterattack.*

Leandro launched at Sebi. Instead of backing, Sebi moved into the attack. His blade flailed wide. Leandro's blade hit Sebi hard in the shoulder, hard enough to knock him a few steps backwards. He stopped only two paces from Francesca and Catalina.

The crowd cheered.

"Halt!" called the officiant.

Leandro and Sebi's chests heaved as they caught their breath.

"Point, Leandro," Henri said. "That's La Belle, gentlemen."

La Belle, the *beautiful point*, meant that the score was tied, and the next point would take the match. The crowd erupted.

"Sebi!" called Catalina.

He turned and their eyes met.

Francesca had never seen Catalina more beautiful and ethereal than in that moment. Tears made her dark eyes luminous. Her raven hair framed her face and twilight made her skin glow in warm toffee hues. She shook her head. "Stop, please. For me."

A grimace of agony and desperation swept across Sebi's face.

Then Burckhardt stepped into the ring and all attention was drawn to him.

"This is a laugh, a joke!" he roared. "This is how boys settle an argument, not men." Then he tossed two sharps to the ground in the center of the ring.

An electric shock rippled through the crowd.

Francesca's heart thundered in her chest. The heat left her body.

Catalina gave a cry just as the crowd began to chant, "First blood, first blood, first blood."

Sebi and Leandro stared at each other for a long moment, then, simultaneously, they dove for the weapons.

"No! Stop!" yelled Francesca. She rushed forward, but someone grabbed her arm and jerked her back.

Catalina struggled to pull free from someone else's grasp.

Francesca saw Phillip among the crowd a few paces away. She caught his eye. "Find Papa! Now!" she cried.

He nodded and pushed through the throng.

Sebi and Leandro stood with blades ready, bodies tensed for action, the officiant between them. "Gentlemen," he said. "If you are agreed, then the bout will go to first blood."

Leandro and Sebi each gave him a curt nod.

"The first to draw blood on the other will be declared the winner. I expect a fair fight." He stepped back, out of the way and called, *"Allay!"*

Sebi flew at Leandro immediately, his rapier aimed at Leandro's heart. Leandro turned the blade aside and counter attacked. Sebi parried too late, but leapt back, just out of the blade's reach. They regrouped and circled, catching their breath.

The crowd pressed inward, humming with anticipation and nervous excitement.

Francesca's body locked into a knot of tension. She yelled for them to stop, but her voice was swallowed by the clamor. Next to her, Catalina trembled, fingers pressed against her mouth.

Sebi stopped across the ring from Francesca and Catalina. His eyes narrowed. Leandro, back to Francesca, dropped his telltale right shoulder.

Sebi immediately attacked with a *fleche*, leaping toward Leandro, sword arm extended.

Leandro dodged left and avoided Sebi's hurtling body and blade. Leandro swung his rapier toward Sebi's back as he passed.

Sebi twisted and got his own blade around just in time to block the cut to his back. But he was off balance and tripped directly in front of Francesca and Catalina.

Sebi struggled awkwardly to face Leandro.

In slow motion, it seemed, Leandro performed a perfect *bulestra*—a cut time attack. Leandro took a short leap forward, slapping his front foot on the ground.

Sebastian stumbled, sword to one side as he tried to catch his balance.

Francesca screamed and yanked against the hands around her arms but couldn't break loose.

Catalina wrenched free of the boy who held her.

Leandro lunged as Catalina threw herself in front of Sebi.

Francesca's throat contracted, strangling off her scream.

Catalina's body gave a sickening spasm as the sword pierced her ribcage.

Leandro rocked back and cried out in shock.

Sebastian dropped his blade.

Catalina hovered a moment, surprise on her face, hands to her ribs, then Sebi caught her as she collapsed.

The hands on Francesca's arms released. World warping around her, she stumbled forward.

Sebi eased Catalina to the ground and cradled her in his arms. Blood spread across her slender stomach and down her side, pooling on the ground beneath her.

Francesca fell to her knees beside Catalina and fought down hysteria. She took Catalina's hand. "It's all right, Catalina. You'll be fine. I know it." She had to believe it.

Leandro dropped his sword, raised both hands to his head and clutched his hair. "Oh, God! I didn't mean … Oh, God!"

"Catalina, Catalina!" Sebi cried.

Catalina's mouth formed words, but all that came out was a crackling cough. She tried again. "Sebi," she whispered.

Sebi cast stricken eyes at Francesca kneeling beside them. "Do something!" he screamed.

The world wavered around Francesca, and her mind felt mired in place.

What would the signora do?

Stop the bleeding!

Her hands shook as she pressed them against the wound.

Oh God! So much blood. Catalina's blood.

Francesca looked up at the throng of young men. "Fetch Signora Bianchi!" She heard the desperation in her own voice.

Leandro's image rippled through her tears, hands to his pallid face. "Leandro! Give me your shirt!"

"Oh God! God!" he muttered. After a second, the words sunk in and he ripped off the shirt, sending buttons flying.

Catalina moaned when Francesca pressed the fabric against the wound. Red leeched outward and spread across the bandage in no time. Catalina coughed and red flecked her lips.

Despair filled Francesca. The sword must have pierced a lung. Oh God, no! No! "Stay with me, Catalina." urged Francesca through her tears.

I'll wake up. Any moment I'll wake up.

Catalina coughed more blood and gasped for air. "Can't..." She put a hand to her throat.

"Hold this! She needs air," she hissed to Sebi, indicating Leandro's shirt. Sebi pressed on the bandage as Francesca frantically fumbled with the knot on Catalina's bodice, her fingers trembling wildly. Finally, it came loose, and the laces slackened. Catalina took a deep breath and coughed again, flecks of blood bright red against her blue tinged lips. Her face had gone white.

Sebi held her, an unsteady hand pressed to her bandage. "Please, please, Catalina, please." Tears streamed down his face.

She smiled at him. "I saved you," she whispered.

"Oh God, I'm so sorry. I should have listened. I should have stopped," whispered Sebi. "I love you, Catalina."

Catalina's chest heaved as she struggled for air.

"It will be all right." Francesca's voice trembled. She wished it were true. She took Catalina's hand. "Hold on. The signora will come. She'll fix this."

Catalina tried to speak, but coughed more blood and gasped.

"I need you," Francesca murmured. "I love you."

Catalina squeezed her hand. Her eyes closed and she exhaled.

A moment of awful silence descended. Catalina's chest did not rise again.

"No! Catalina! No!" cried Sebi.

Francesca howled with pain. She pressed Catalina's limp hand to her cheek and squeezed, willing the life back into it. The world tilted and spun in waves. Pieces of her crumbled to nothingness.

Then Signora Bianchi was there beside Sebi checking Catalina's pulse.

Papa lifted Francesca to her feet.

"Signora," he said, "Is there anything to be done?"

"I'm sorry, Maestro. Catalina's gone."

Sebi barked out a sob as he rocked her body.

"Antonio," said Papa, nodding toward Sebi.

Antonio knelt beside Sebi and wrapped an arm around his brother.

As Papa turned Francesca away, she saw Burckhardt six paces off, his eyes intent on Catalina. Francesca's pain erupted into rage. She flared into fiery, unreasoning hate. "You did this!" she screamed. "It's your fault!"

She shook free of Papa's hands, scooped up Sebi's blade lying at her feet, and lunged toward Burckhardt.

Papa caught her around the waist.

Burckhardt backed away, his face red and his eyes burning.

Francesca twisted to get free, to get at Burckhardt.

"Stop, Francesca! Stop!" yelled Papa. He held her tight with one arm and tried to pry the sword out of her hand with the other. "That's enough!"

Francesca released the blade as the fire raging through her core was doused by an avalanche of cold grief. She turned to Papa and crushed her face into his shoulder. Her keening wail seemed to fill the whole world.

Papa raised his voice to the crowd of young men. "Everyone to your rooms! This second! You're to stay there until we get to the bottom of this."

He turned to Signora Bianchi and Antonio. "Signora, please see to Catalina. Antonio, help your brother inside."

Then Papa wrapped his arms tight around Francesca and rocked her.

CHAPTER 16
FOR BETTER OR FOR WORSE

Francesca sat on her bed, curled into a ball. She held her arms tight around her body as she rocked and sobbed, trying to keep from flying to pieces. She didn't know how much time had passed, how long she had wept, but it seemed like forever. Her throat felt raw. She ached with sorrow, with longing for her friend, and with regret at everything Catalina would never experience.

Signora Bianchi spoke softly to Francesca and put a hand on her shoulder or arm now and then. For once, her presence was comforting and Francesca was grateful.

When Francesca ran out of tears and her sobs subsided, the signora took a handkerchief from her pocket and wiped Francesca's cheeks, and then her own cheeks, splotched red and tear stained.

"Now then," the signora blew her nose and gave Francesca a weak smile. "We must be strong for Catalina's sake, mustn't we?"

Francesca nodded mechanically, though she didn't see why. Catalina was gone. What did it matter if they were strong or not? It would change nothing.

"It's very late." Her governess glanced at the black square of the window. "Try to get some rest. Would you like me to help you with your laces or bring you some laudanum to help you sleep?"

Francesca shook her head. "Thank you, signora, but I'll manage."

"As you wish," the signora rose, but hesitated, as if reluctant to leave. At last, she sat down on the bed again, gave Francesca a fierce lingering hug, then left.

Francesca unraveled from the ball she'd curled herself into and rose from the bed. How could loss cause so much pain? Her whole body hurt, as if she'd fallen from a great height.

She went to the window and looked out. Beyond the black slash of the stone wall that enclosed the courtyard, a crescent moon glittered blue off the leaves of the great elm over the dueling grounds. A spike entered her heart. She put her hand to her chest.

Her eyes swung to the stable. This was to have been her and Phillip's wedding night. This should have been the happiest night of her life. Was Phillip out there, right now, waiting for her?

Suddenly all she wanted to do was run. She wanted to fling herself on Achilles' back and gallop away from the horror of what had happened— away from the helplessness and terrible pain. She wanted to fly and never stop, and she wanted Phillip with her, his arms around her, the warmth of his body, his voice in her ear.

She knelt and felt under her bed for the bag she'd filled earlier. Was that only a few hours ago? It seemed like a lifetime. She dragged the bag out, hefted it over her shoulder, blew out the candle, and, without a look back, slipped out the door.

The courtyard shone after the dark hall and stairs. The cold air bit at her exposed skin. She paused only a moment to scan the area before she headed for the main gate.

She intended to head for the stable and Achilles, but instead, her feet took her behind the stable to the dueling grounds.

An icy breeze rustled the leaves of the giant sentinel elm and raised goosebumps on her skin. She dropped her bag at her feet. She stepped forward carefully, eyes scanning the ground. Catalina's shoe appeared, and Leandro's bloody shirt she'd used to try to stop the bleeding, and there, the dark spot where Catalina's life had bled into the soil.

Francesca sank to her knees.

As clearly as if Catalina had leaned down and whispered in her ear, she heard Catalina's voice, "My God Francesca, what have you done?"

Francesca's breath shuddered, and she swayed.

What have I done!

She bent forward as her stomach heaved, but there was nothing to bring up. She put a hand on the cold ground to brace herself.

Oh God! It wasn't Burckhardt or Leandro.

I told Sebi to challenge Leandro.

If not for me, none of them would have been there. I did this. I killed her!

Francesca slumped to the ground on her side.

Why couldn't I leave things be? Catalina wanted to help her family! She was sad, but she wanted to marry Leandro for them. She was such a good person, a hundred, a thousand times better than me. I should be the one who's dead.

She longed to trade places with Catalina.

All I've ever done has been for myself.

Francesca covered her face with her hands and shook her head. The breeze filtered through the leaves, rubbing them together until they hissed and swished and words emerged. *"Sssel … fffffish, ssel ffffish, sselfffish,"* over and over.

She couldn't breathe. She was suffocating. Which seemed right. She should die. She wanted the earth to open and swallow her. How could she live with what she had done? She clawed at the dirt, willing it to cover her.

"Selfffish," murmured the leaves.

Other memories flooded back.

Catalina on the stairs, angry, saying, "Have you heard nothing your father has said about honor?"

Sebi staring at her and shaking his head. "You are an evil little minx, aren't you?"

Her fault.

How could she have heard without hearing? How could she have been so blinded by her own petty concerns? She tore at her clothing.

Was there anyone at the salle she'd never lied to or manipulated?

"Selfffish," said the breeze and the giant elm.

Achilles was the only one she'd ever been completely honest with. She'd lied to all of them, continually, Papa and Signora Bianchi most of all. Her dishonor had brought her here. She deserved to be the one lying dead, not Catalina.

To defend God and country. To keep one's word. To avoid lying and cheating. To exhibit courage in word and deed. To live for freedom, justice, and all that is good. To die with honor. How could she have said those words so many times without understanding them once? They weren't rules to limit her freedom, they were guides to save her from this pain, from the soul-crushing regret that swallowed her. She had tried to cheat Catalina's parents, Leandro, and his family, all to arrange things for herself. If she'd acted honorably, Catalina would still live.

"Selfffish, selfffish,"

"Stop! Stop!" Francesca yelled up into the branches overhead.

"Francesca?"

It was Phillip's voice.

Francesca gave a guttural cry.

Moments later Phillip knelt beside her. She could make out little of his face, but she knew the feel and smell of him, the comfort of his arms.

"Francesca, are you all right?"

"No," she gasped as he eased her shoulders up into his arms. "Oh, Phillip, nothing will ever be right again."

"I'm so sorry about Catalina," he said. "I came out just in case, in case you needed me."

She clutched him tightly. "I do need you, Phillip. I need you. It's my fault she's dead."

"You didn't stab her." Phillip cradled her. She clung to his warmth.

"I might as well have."

"Don't say that. You loved Catalina. I know you did."

Francesca nodded.

Phillip put a hand to her cheek. "We can still get away from here. We can put this all behind us and start new. I love you, Francesca."

Francesca's heart leapt. She wanted more than anything to fly, to make all the pain go away, but then she heard the leaves overhead.

"Oh, Phillip," she gasped. "I can't go."

"Of course you can." Phillip smoothed her hair. "There's nothing to it. We saddle the horses and ride away."

"But Papa," Francesca said. "He'd be heartbroken. And Signora Bianchi, I know she's hard sometimes, but she loves me. I can't do that to them."

"But Francesca—"

"I can't leave Sebi now. He's lost his love. He may hate me, but he'll still need me. And I can't let him and Leandro take all the blame."

She gave a hiccupping cry. "And I can't do that to you, Phillip. I love you. I want to be with you, but I can't let you give up so much for me."

"I'm not giving up anything important," Phillip said. "Only you matter."

Phillip's fingers touched the bare skin of her arm. "Good Lord, Francesca, you're freezing. Let's get you up off this damp ground."

Phillip rose and helped her up. Her legs wobbled and she leaned against him. He rubbed her arms to warm them.

"Maybe you don't care about your future now," Francesca said, wiping tears from her face. "But what about five years from now, or twenty years? Someday you'll resent all you gave up for me."

"No, Francesca."

"I tricked you into fencing with me. I nearly got you expelled. I don't deserve your love, Phillip. You should hate me. I've been so selfish. I haven't cared who I hurt as long as I got what I wanted."

Phillip wrapped his arms around her and rocked her. "Hush," he said. "I fenced with you because I chose to. You couldn't have made me if I hadn't wanted to. Besides, what does it matter how, as long as we fell in love?"

"I do love you, Phillip, with all my heart," she said. "That's why I can't go with you."

He shook his head. "That makes no sense."

"It does. It's because I love you that I can't let you dishonor your name, as I have."

"Francesca—"

"Please, Phillip. You have to go home and do as your father commands."

Phillip turned away. "If I go home," he said bitterly, "it's to challenge him for killing my mother."

Francesca's heart twisted with new pain. How could she refuse him and send him to possible death? She couldn't be responsible for more loss.

She put a hand on his shoulder. "No, Phillip, no. You said yourself he didn't kill her. That she, she made a choice. You can't kill your father over a choice someone else made. That's not justice, it's revenge."

"But he drove her to it."

"Like I drove Sebi to challenge Leandro," Francesca said, her voice thick with fresh tears.

Phillip took her hands. "No, it's not the same. You're not to blame for Catalina's death. Sebi and Leandro chose to pick up those sharps. Catalina chose to leap in front of Sebi."

Francesca took a deep breath as the weight of the guilt on her shoulders lightened a fraction. "And your mother chose, too," she said softly.

Phillip looked away. "The man is violent and greedy. Why should I do as he says?"

"Because it's your duty," Francesca said. Her voice shook as she added, "Catalina tried to teach me how important that is, but I wouldn't listen."

"But the man has no honor!"

"It's not about him. It's about you. If you give up your honor, you become him."

Phillip was silent.

She held him tight against her, her heart torn to pieces. She'd lost her best friend, and now she was losing Phillip as well.

"If this is what you really want, I'll leave in the morning," he said, his voice raw and filled with pain.

Francesca gave a sob and shook her head. "No, Phillip, it's the last thing in the world that I want, but it's the way it has to be."

Tears dripped from her chin as she held him. She listened to his heartbeat and wondered if it was possible to hear a heart break.

When bouts of trembling overcame Francesca in waves, they retreated to the warmth of the stable. They piled hay in the corner of Achilles's stall then lay together in the dark, wrapped in each other's arms. Francesca wished the morning would never come.

Too soon, light crept in around the stable door and the horses began to stir. She rose and brushed hay from her clothes and hair. She watched Phillip. Relaxed in sleep, he was almost too beautiful for words. How she loved the curve of his lips, the red softness of his cheeks now grazed with golden stubble, his tousled hair. She longed to snuggle beneath his arm and rest her face in the hollow of his collarbone laid bare by his rumpled shirt. She couldn't bear to wake him from his peace into the loss that awaited him, but it wouldn't do for them to be found together.

Numb with loss, she crept from the stable into a pearlescent dawn and the cheerful chirps of songbirds. They seemed to mock her.

She was drawn to the dueling grounds as if by a string tied right below her heart.

The blades Sebi and Leandro had used lay where they'd been dropped, dark blood now crusted along one of their edges. They were Burckhardt's blades. She'd seen them in his possession. Papa had ordered everyone into the salle, so Burckhardt hadn't had a chance to collect them.

Though Catalina's body had been taken away, Francesca felt her presence, her calm, happy energy, and that made the ache in Francesca's heart even worse.

I'm sorry Catalina, she thought. *I am so terribly, horribly sorry. You were right. About everything.*

Francesca knelt where Catalina had died.

I'll bring flowers every day.

"I didn't kill her."

Burckhardt's voice made Francesca jump.

He strode from around the stable. His chin was thrust forward and his hands balled into fists. "You want me to hang for that girl's stupidity."

Francesca jumped to her feet, anger flaring. She hated the look of him, the thought of him, everything about him. "You brought the sharps! No one needed to get hurt!"

"Practice blades are for cowards and weaklings, like your brother." Burckhardt advanced toward her. "Weeping over that girl."

Francesca looked down at Catalina's dried blood. How dare he defile this spot.

"Go away!" she yelled.

"I intend to, but not without my blades." Burckhardt leaned down and picked up the sword caked with Catalina's blood. He stepped toward her.

"Stay away from me!" she growled.

"You were pretty keen on getting close to me yesterday, when I was unarmed," he said.

Francesca glanced at the other blade lying a few feet away. Her rage turned ice cold. She wanted more than anything to pick up the blade and plunge it into Burckhardt's gut, but there had been enough death.

He smiled. "Maybe I'll just cut up that pretty face of yours. We'll see what Worthington thinks of you then."

Francesca rose and backed. "You wouldn't strike an unarmed woman."

"Wouldn't I?"

"You can't." Fear crept in around the edges of her anger.

"Who are you to tell me what I can and cannot do? You're nothing. Less than nothing. The daughter of a servant."

Burckhardt picked up the second rapier. "I'll tell them that you attacked me and I defended myself. There are plenty who witnessed your attack last night. But it works better..." He tossed the rapier at Francesca, and she instinctively caught it. "...If you're armed." And he came at her.

Burckhardt attacked, swinging his blade high and wide, thundering.

Her body reacted before her brain could object. She dropped low, blade arm extended and the tip held waist-high.

Burckhardt's blade slashed far above her head. He skidded to a halt, bent double over the tip of Francesca's blade, which just touched his stomach. A spot of red appeared.

He backed off and cursed. "You bloody little jezebel!"

"That's first blood." Francesca rose. "That's enough. We're done."

"This isn't a duel, it's punishment." Burckhardt sneered.

He attacked again, tip aimed at her face. She parried, but his rapier skimmed across her shoulder. She felt the fabric of her sleeve give and blood flow.

The sting sharpened her mind and for a moment, all the pain of last night fell away.

He attacked again. She parried and reposted, drawing a line of blood across his forearm.

Burckhardt roared with rage and attacked wildly. Francesca parried each stroke as she backed away.

She fought the urge to attack. She couldn't kill a nobleman. Even seriously injuring him might land her in prison.

Burckhardt's attacks came harder and harder, until he swung his blade at her like a club. She turned each blow aside or dodged out of the way.

Finally, Francesca waited for his attack, then corkscrewed her blade around his, twisting the hilt from his grasp. His rapier flew through the air.

Burckhardt cursed.

Francesca sidestepped, following the tumbling blade. When it landed on the ground, she stood over it and faced him. Burckhardt brought himself up short when he stood unarmed, facing Francesca's blade.

She smiled. She could lunge now and kill him, but he wasn't worth it.

Antonio rushed around the corner of the stable and paused as he took in the scene.

He looked at her in confusion. "I heard blades. I thought Sebi and Leandro might be fighting again. What's going on? Why is your arm bleeding?"

Francesca shrugged. "Poor point control. He was aiming for my face. It's nothing."

Antonio hurtled toward Burckhardt, who backed away, hands up.

Antonio shoved Burckhardt hard, then grabbed him roughly by the upper arm. "If your aim had been true, I would have killed you right here." He shoved Burckhardt back toward the main gate.

Papa, panting for breath, appeared from around the stable as well. He sighed with relief when he saw Antonio haul Burckhardt away as Francesca stood over his blade. He put a hand to his chest. "I saw from my office window. I thought he might kill you. Or you might kill him."

Francesca shook her head. "He's a small man, despite his size. He has to live with the fact that he was beaten by a girl, twice."

She lowered her blade at last. "Burckhardt didn't kill Catalina. I did." Her voice shook and her chin trembled as she fought back tears. "It was all my fault."

"No, Cesca." Papa moved toward her. "Leandro held the blade. Sebastian challenged him. Burckhardt escalated the duel." He stopped in front of her.

"But I convinced Sebi to challenge Leandro," Francesca said. Shame welled up and tears streamed down her face. "I was selfish. I didn't want her to go. I behaved," she sobbed, "dishonorably."

"Ah, my dear," Papa said, gently but firmly, "It wasn't *all* your fault. There is more than enough blame to go around. But you were involved, you did act dishonorably, and that is something you're going to have to find a way to live with."

She nodded. *How can I live with this much pain?*

Papa reached to take the blade from her hand, but she took a step back and tightened her grip on the hilt.

Papa's face darkened. "Francesca, give me the blade."

Her voice cracked as she said, "No, Papa. I won't."

His voice took on an edge she had never heard. "Give me the sword."

Francesca shook her head, her throat too thick for words. She tightened her grip on the sword, then turned on her heels and ran.

CHAPTER 17
LESSONS

Francesca ran out from under the trees into the bright sun of the sheep pasture. Grasses ripped at her skirts, and Papa called her name behind her. Startled sheep looked up at her, then went back to munching grass. When she reached the far side of the pasture, she glanced back at Papa still standing beneath the trees, then followed the footpath into the woods.

By the time Francesca reached her favorite climbing tree, she gasped for breath. She sat on the fallen limb and put a hand to the stitch in her side. She looked at Burckhardt's sword still in her other hand. She pulled her arm back to throw it away, but she couldn't.

She knew what Catalina would say, so she said it for her—mimicking Catalina's exasperated tone. "What was running supposed to accomplish?"

Francesca put her free hand to her heart and kneaded the ache. She closed her eyes. *I miss you.*

Francesca rose. She explained to Catalina as she walked farther along the path, using the sword as a walking stick. "I ran because I was scared. I was afraid that Papa wouldn't love me anymore if I told him the truth. If I told him all that I've done and all that I want."

She stopped beside the stream where she and Sebi had played as kids. Then it had been the mighty Amazon or the crocodile-infested Nile. Today there was merely a trickle of water that splashed between moss-covered rocks. She turned right and followed the stream to the spot where she and

Sebi had rolled rocks into the creek to create a small pool. She picked up a stone and tossed it in, watching the ripples spread and echo back and forth.

She walked on until she reached the tumbling stone barn where she'd played as a child and had played at fencing with Phillip.

Francesca leaned against the cool grey stone wall.

The time had come to leave childhood behind. If only she'd done it sooner, Catalina might still be with her. Time to pick up the responsibilities she'd worked so hard and for so long to avoid. Realizing she'd been selfish and deceitful wasn't enough, she had to do something about it.

Papa.

She looked at the sword. He had to know who she was. He had to see. She had to speak the truth, no matter the consequences. Even if it meant losing him, her home, all she had left. "I won't live a lie anymore," she said.

Francesca imagined a smile quirking Catalina's lips as she said, "It's about time."

She turned toward home.

———

When she passed the stable outside the main gate, she saw Phillip on Iago a dozen yards down the road heading away from the salle. *No!*

He had said he would. She knew he had to leave, but she wasn't ready. She couldn't bear it.

"Phillip!" she called.

He reined in Iago and turned to her. Filled with sorrow and longing, she committed every detail to memory—the curve of his jaw, his tousled golden hair, and his piercing blue eyes. Francesca couldn't think of anything more to say. She'd said everything last night in the stable. She just needed to see him.

He looked back for a long moment, then smiled. "We'll see each other again." He put a hand to his heart. "I know it." Then he urged Iago on and continued down the hill.

She watched his form recede for a long time. She envied his hope. All she felt was a growing hollow space in her heart as she climbed the stairs.

As Francesca walked toward her room, Sebi emerged from his doorway. Francesca froze.

Sebi was unshaven and unkempt, his shoulders hunched. He stopped dead when he saw Francesca. His sore, red eyes hardened, and his jaw clenched. Without a word he went back into his room and shut the door.

Francesca put a hand on the wall to steady herself. Would he ever forgive her? Could she ever forgive herself?

In her room, Francesca set the sword on her bed and stared at it for a long time.

Courage. Honor. Integrity. She'd played at them in the past, like a child plays at tea. Time to make them hers, or perhaps make herself theirs. She had to live her life by those principles so nothing like Catalina's death would ever happen again.

She took a deep breath, sat at her desk, and pulled out paper and ink.

First, she wrote a letter to Catalina's mother, detailing what had happened and how horribly sorry she was for her part in it. She wrote about what a wonderful friend and caring person Catalina had been and how much she would miss her calm, wise spirit.

The next letter was to Papa. When she finished it, she took the note and Burckhardt's sword and headed downstairs to Papa's office.

Francesca stood in front of the oak door and raised her hand to knock. But her hand stopped midair. Once she passed through that door her life would be changed forever. She stood with eyes closed and heart pounding.

"To keep one's word. To defend the weak and innocent. To never abandon a noble cause. To avoid lying and cheating. To exhibit courage in word and deed," she whispered. She straightened her shoulders and rapped.

"Come," said Papa's voice.

He rose from his desk when she entered. "Francesca." He frowned, his voice tight.

Signora Bianchi sat in a leather chair, her long hands folded on her lap. Her eyes, focused on Francesca, looked red and sore.

Francesca stepped into his office as if into a confessional. "Papa, I need to talk to you, and to Signora Bianchi too." Francesca crossed the room and laid Burkhardt's blade on the desk. Papa took the blade and set it back behind his desk.

"Very well." Papa sat back down.

"We're listening," said the signora.

Francesca paced from bookcase to bookcase, unsure how to begin. There was so much she needed to say, and so much she dreaded telling. *Start with Phillip.*

She took a deep breath, then told Papa and the signora all that had passed between her and Phillip.

Papa ran his hands down his face, and the signora huffed and shook her head through much of it.

Then she told them of their plans to elope.

Papa and the signora rose from their seats shouting at her.

Francesca, emotionally spent, only caught bits. The look of naked fear on Papa's face as he yelled, "I might have lost you forever!" The signora shouting, "You could have been ruined!" Papa saying, "Shudder to think what his father might have done." "Would have been penniless," from the signora.

Finally, she held up both hands. "I couldn't do it," said Francesca. "I couldn't. I knew how hurt you would be and how dishonorable it was. But, oh Papa, I love him!" Tears ran down her cheeks. "And he accepted me, the real me, when none of the rest of you did."

Papa and the signora fell silent.

She went on as her anger rose. "Phillip loved fencing with me, and he loved that I wasn't a milquetoast maid who waited to be rescued. I never had to pretend around him like I had to around you. He loved me for who I was, not for who he wanted me to be."

She turned to the signora. "You said no man would want a wife who could fence. Well, Phillip did. I found a man who would have given up a fortune and a title for me. And I sent him away, because it was the honorable thing to do. Because that's what Catalina would have done."

Crimson flamed the signora's cheeks.

Francesca went on. "I won't be that girl anymore, I won't lie. I won't weasel my way to what I want and pretend to be someone I'm not to make others happy. I can't live like that any longer."

The signora smoothed her skirts. "I'm sorry, Francesca. Perhaps I was wrong, but I did what I thought best. I meant to make your life easier."

"You tried to lock me in the convent," Francesca said.

"Yes, but I never intended for you to spend more than a few days. I thought seeing how restrictive life was at Colleviti would make you feel freer here."

Only a few days? Francesca huffed in surprise and shock. Perhaps things might have turned out differently if she'd spent a couple days with the nuns instead of accusing Burckhardt.

"Still, Maestro," said the signora, "we must consider her reputation. What's to be done?"

"Done?" Papa said. "Phillip may have been misguided, but he is an honorable lad. I believe her reputation is safe."

The signora's shoulders relaxed. "That relieves my mind."

Papa shook his head and turned to Francesca. "But I never asked you to pretend to be someone else."

Francesca's cheeks flamed with anger. "But you did, Papa! You demanded it!"

Pain mixed with anger on his face, and he stood. "You've misunderstood."

"No, Papa. You did. All I ever wanted was to fence, and you forbid me even to ask!"

"Yes, Francesca. Because for you, fencing was a game, a dance." He flung a hand toward the window, toward the spot where Catalina had died. "It is anything but. The one and only purpose of a sword is to kill."

His eyes bored into hers, and she fought back a sob.

"Each and every young man here may be called upon by God, by king and country, or by honor to take up a sword and kill or die. That is the reason—the only reason—I try to give them all the skill I have."

He ran a hand down his face. "Poor Leandro. There is no greater pain than taking a life. It can destroy a man's soul unless he knows that he had no choice, that his actions were demanded of him. That is why I teach honor. Honor dictates our actions. If a man kills honorably then that action was necessary and he is blameless."

Francesca imagined what Leandro must be going through. She heard the signora sniffle.

"Cesca, there is no part of this I want for you. What if you had killed Burckhardt, even accidentally? The law is clear; a woman who kills a man will be hung. Do you understand? Hung!"

"I understand, Papa. I see what you wanted to protect me from. I know now what a sword is. I understand the responsibility." She swallowed the lump in her throat. She looked back and forth between Papa and Signora Bianchi. "But this is who I am."

"Francesca, I—" Papa said.

She raised her hand. "That day, Papa. All those years ago, when you forbid me to ask."

Papa frowned and nodded.

Her voice shook. "I've fenced alone in my room every day since."

She couldn't look at him, but she heard his sharp, indrawn breath as well as Signora Bianchi's.

"I, I wanted—"

"Cesca!"

She turned back to him. His face was taut with anger.

She couldn't stop. "At first, I wanted to fence to be close to you. Then when Phillip came, and…" She searched for words as she looked away from the fury in his face. "And when I fenced against a real opponent, I came alive for the first time. Nothing else mattered." She wiped her cheeks. "After we were caught, I tried to stop. I tried, Papa. But there was nothing left once it was gone. I was a shell." She dropped her head. "I'll understand if you can never forgive me."

She shook her head and called up all her resolve. She needed to be worthy of his love, and of Catalina's. "There are two paths forward for me, Papa. I know which I would choose, but my duty is to obey you." She had told Phillip as much when she sent him away. "If you order me to never touch a blade again, I swear, on Catalina's soul, I'll obey. But…" She took a few breaths, trying unsuccessfully to steady her voice.

Papa stepped toward her, face red, eyebrows lowered.

"But if I can't fence, I can't stay here," she said. "I won't be part of this family. I can't watch you, and Sebi, and Antonio fence. I can't listen to the talk, hear the blades, I can't…" Her throat clogged.

She turned toward the window, toward the towering elm. She forced out, "I'll go to Colleviti."

She shivered.

"There are no temptations there, no way for me to dishonor myself, and I have enough sins to atone for." How would she ever atone for what she'd done to Catalina?

The signora let out a breath.

It seemed like an eternity that she stood there, head bowed, heart full of pain.

Finally, Papa put a firm hand on her shoulder and turned her toward him. His face was stiff, his eyes like gray chips of stone.

"Nine years! For nine years you've disobeyed me and lied to me. I don't know what to say." He turned away.

There was a roaring in Francesca's ears. Her vision narrowed as darkness crept in around the edges. She'd thought she was prepared to accept the consequences, but she wasn't. Could anyone be prepared to lose their father's love?

Now Papa paced quickly to the bookcase and back again. Once, twice, three times, his shoulders tense, his face tight.

She bent over, hands on her knees. There didn't seem to be enough air.

The signora watched with one hand over her mouth.

Papa's pacing slowed. "I should have seen," Papa said. He stopped and looked at her again. "I didn't want to know." He paced again.

Francesca concentrated on drawing air into her lungs and expelling it.

Papa stopped again, closer this time. He spoke distantly. "The signs were there. The muscle development, the reflexes, the knowledge. I lied to myself." He looked away. "I spent so much time with the boys. It was easier, clearer, I knew what to do."

As he turned to her, some of his anger drained away. After a pause he asked, "What is the second path?"

Francesca drew the letter from her pocket and handed it to him. He unfolded it and read. "Four o'clock, dairy, check daily supplies, four-thirty, meet shipment from Cascina, five to seven help with breakfast, eight o'clock Latin…" He looked at her. "What is this? Your punishment?"

"No, Papa, if I'm going to stay here then this is the life I want. It's time I was lady of the house in more than name. It's the schedule and duties of a head housekeeper."

The signora gasped.

Papa's eyebrows rose in surprise. "This is a big change in attitude."

"I know, Papa. It's long overdue. But I want this. I want my life here at the salle to mean something. I've realized how much everyone here has given me, and it is high time I started giving back. This is the best way I can think of to do it."

Papa glanced from her to the signora and back. "Do you think you're ready?"

"I am." She nodded to the signora. "Signora Bianchi and Signora Morello were good teachers, even if they had a reluctant pupil. And Signora Morello can finally retire, as she's wanted." She turned to the signora and took her hand. "I can do it. If Elena will help me, as an advisor and a friend."

The signora's chin began to wobble, and her eyes filled with tears. She squeezed Francesca's hand. "Of course, my dear."

"But Papa," said Francesca. "There's one addition, in the evening."

He scanned the paper. "Seven o'clock, fencing lesson in the schoolroom."

He crumpled the paper and dropped it. Francesca's heart crumpled with it.

"I taught your mother to fence." Papa looked off into the distance. He shook his head and focused on Francesca. "If I hadn't, she might still be alive. I swore I'd never teach another woman."

He puffed out a breath. "And I don't like ultimatums, Francesca. I make the decisions for this family." He nodded toward the crumpled paper. "These are fine words, but why should I believe you if you've been lying to me for this long?"

"Because I've killed my best friend, Papa. I've taken from this world the kindest, most honorable person I know. I can't change it. I can't undo it. All I can do to make up for it is to be as honorable and kind as she was."

Pain crossed his face, and he made the sign of the cross. "Let me think on it." He pointed at the door. "Now go!"

———†———

The next morning, at four o'clock, Francesca wrapped a shawl around her shoulders and headed to the dairy. Papa hadn't forbidden her to take over the housekeeper's duties, so she would, unless ordered otherwise. If Papa wanted proof that she meant what she said, she would give it to him.

In the warm, pungent air of the barn, Iris, a white and brown cow, lowed and shook her head. Theresa, one of the milkmaids, patted Iris on the back. "She and Clover are both ill," said Theresa.

"Poor girls." Francesca rubbed Iris's ear. "Is there anything we can do?"

"No, they'll be fine, but please let Chef know we'll be short on milk for the next few days."

"I will." She scratched Clover on the jowls. "And I'll check on you tomorrow."

After she relayed the message to Chef Amico, Francesca and Signora Morello met the butcher's delivery cart and oversaw stowing the meat in the cellar. Then she was back in the kitchen to help with breakfast.

The day flew by. Signora Morello was grateful for Francesca's help and gave her an unexpected hug, burying Francesca's face in the woman's ample bosom.

When dinner time came Francesca grabbed a few bites in the kitchen. She had no appetite, and she couldn't face a family meal sitting across from Sebi and Papa.

At seven in the evening, she grabbed a practice foil and went to the schoolroom. She hoped to find Papa waiting for her, but the room was empty. She wiped away tears as she tucked up her skirts and started her footwork. She practiced for an hour, glancing at the doorway every few minutes. Her heart sank a bit more each time it stood vacant.

One evening about two weeks later, Francesca worked under the giant elm with a spade. Papa had closed the dueling grounds, so she had gotten permission to turn the spot into a garden in Catalina's honor.

She paused and wiped the sweat from her forehead with the back of her hand. Birds sang overhead. The evening sun turned the landscape golden orange. The smell of the damp, loamy soil spoke of growth and renewal.

She had just gone back to shoveling when Sebi appeared, spade in hand. Without a word, he started working alongside her. Francesca slid her shovel into the earth, lifted and turned. She didn't dare say anything for fear of chasing him away. They worked on in silence.

"Irises were her favorite," Sebi said.

"Yes," Francesca said. "And roses."

They worked some more.

"We should bring one of the benches from the garden," Sebi said.

"We should." Francesca looked over at him and smiled. He smiled back.

A month passed in a flash.

Francesca was worn out, but she was getting used to her new routine. Up at four each morning for work and school, she still managed to sneak in a ride each afternoon before eating dinner in the kitchen. After that, she had lonely fencing practice in the schoolroom. She was glad that at least she hadn't been forbidden to practice, and that she had more space in the schoolroom than in her bedroom. Then she did schoolwork and chores until she fell into bed exhausted each night.

She was surprised how challenging and engaging she found managing the salle. She liked meeting problems head-on, and she loved being forced to think on her feet and invent new solutions.

Like last week, when she discovered who was stealing the good silverware one piece at a time. She'd put the silverware away in the drawer, then before bed had carefully smeared the back of the drawer handle with tar. She was disappointed in the morning when another piece of silver was missing but all the servants' fingers were clean. Until breakfast, when she told Antonio about her ploy, and he burst out laughing. One of the students had stained fingers that morning. Papa was informed, the silverware returned, and the young man sent home.

Francesca felt proud of her work. She was also earning the respect of the tradesmen and servants, and that felt good too.

As she entered the schoolroom for another lonely practice session, her mind was occupied with thoughts of the next day. She needed to talk to the groundskeeper about expanding the kitchen garden. That would provide more vegetables and herbs for Chef Amico's soup pots and save money by relying less on local vendors. But what exactly should they plant?

She looked up and her heart skipped a beat. "Papa!"

He stood at the far end of the room, hands clasped behind his back.

She'd seen little of him in the past month and a half, mostly on purpose. No news was sometimes good news. Was he here to render judgement? Forbid her to practice? She gripped her practice foil tighter.

"Hello, my Cesca." He stepped forward a few paces. "I've missed you."

"Well, I, I've been busy," she said nervously.

"I know you have. And I'm impressed with the way you've taken over managing things around here."

"Thank you," she said as he moved yet closer.

"And I've been thinking a good deal about what you asked," he continued. "And about your mother."

Her heart sped up and her stomach fluttered. She looked away.

He stood before her. "Your mother would tell me that pirates killed her, not fencing. She would say that the world is a dangerous place, and that she would want our daughter to be able to defend herself."

Her eyes flew to his face where a smile spread. "Your mother would also tell me that she would haunt me 'til the end of my days if I allowed that convent to crush your spirit. For better or for worse, you're part of this family."

"You mean you'll teach me?"

"Yes, my Cesca, I'll teach you."

She threw herself into his arms and kissed him on the cheek. "Thank you, thank you, Papa!"

He released her and ran a hand through his hair. "I don't know what this will mean for your future. Who knows where it will lead, but we'll walk the road together. Above all, you need honor and discipline. I will be hard on you, Francesca, much harder than I've ever been on your brothers. And if you lie to me ever again, it's all over."

"I swear on my life, Papa, I will uphold the code of honor, always."

Papa nodded once. "I know you will." Then he clapped his hands together. "Well, then, let's get to it."

Francesca handed him her foil and tucked the top six inches of her voluminous skirts and petticoats under her stays so she wouldn't trip on them.

"Hmm. We'll have to consider appropriate attire. Perhaps we can shorten one of your skirts and lighten the petticoats. The stays will have to go, and perhaps we can add some padding to the bodice, but this will do for today."

Francesca took a deep breath. Her heart and body thrummed as Papa laid the practice foil in her hand.

She fell into *en garde* position and Papa called the drill. He had her advance, lunge, retreat, *patenando*, *bulestra*. He ran her through the attack lines and parries and had her perform a dozen other moves. When he finally called "Halt" Francesca glowed with effort and happiness.

Papa shook his head in surprise. "Your form is nearly perfect, my Cesca! And you're quick, too. You'll make a fine fencer." He moved to her right side and put his hand over her sword hand. "But you turn your wrist this way," he said, adjusting her position.

Francesca's breath caught.

Sebi and Antonio appeared in the doorway, foils in hand. "Can we join you?" asked Sebi.

"Yes! Oh, yes," she said as tears of joy ran down her cheeks.

NEXT IN THE LADY BLADE SERIES
LADY BLADE

Lady Blade begins three years later. Here is the first chapter as a sample.

CHAPTER 1
DAWN

Francesca DiCesare knew Papa was the best swordsman in all the states of Italy, perhaps all the world, yet she couldn't shake the foreboding that had settled on her as they journeyed toward the dueling grounds.

The gray dawn wasn't helping. The only things visible through the surrounding mist were her two brothers and Papa on their horses, looking colorless and ghostly, and a dozen paces of dirt road. Only a lightening of the haze indicated where the sun rose.

The damp air seeped through the wool of her red cloak thrusting icy fingers up her sleeves and down her collar.

Francesca sat sidesaddle atop her black horse, Achilles. He rumbled deep in his chest, and she rubbed his neck knowing he was disgruntled at being taken from his warm stable so early, and without his morning oats. He tossed his head and snorted.

A few yards ahead rode her two older brothers, Antonio and Sebastian. Antonio, the eldest, tried to joke with Sebi to lighten the mood, but Sebi's replies were half-hearted, and his shoulders hunched.

It was easy to guess what was on his mind—what was on all their minds. The duel he had fought two years ago. That duel had cost Francesca her closest friend, and Sebi his first love.

She tried to keep her thoughts from going to that heart-rending day. Her breath caught as the image arose of Catalina throwing herself in front of Sebi to take the blade that was meant for him. Guilt flooded her for her involvement in the affair. And the blood … *Stop. Just stop. I can't think about it*, she told herself fiercely, *or I'll fall apart completely*.

She took a deep, steadying breath and turned toward Papa, who rode alongside her. The gray mist made his face pallid and lined, highlighting the scars that slanted across his right cheekbone and ran down his broad forehead.

It's just the light, she told herself. *He's not old.* But lately she'd noticed he tried to hide a limp when the weather changed and the old war injury to his thigh acted up. And he'd asked Signora Bianchi for a salve for the arthritis in his shoulder.

There was no hint of worry on his face, though. His back was straight and his expression serene.

Francesca wanted to lay a hand on his arm and say, "Please, Papa, let's go home," but it was pointless. He had been challenged. Now it was a matter of honor, and his honor meant more to him than anything, even his life.

She looked away. *Everything will be fine. He's fought a hundred duels, maybe a thousand. He marched with armies and faced down kings. He always wins.* But she couldn't stop her traitorous mind from adding, *so far.*

Her reluctance had slowed her pace and she had fallen a few paces behind. He turned to her, crinkling his steel-gray eyes and bunching his goatee at the corners of his mouth. "Come along, Cesca, we mustn't be late."

She hurried Achilles' pace.

"Are you sure they can spare you today?" Papa asked.

"Yes, Papa. Signora Elena will meet the deliveries and everyone else has their duties. They'll be fine without me for the morning."

He nodded. "Have I mentioned lately how proud I am of the way you've been running the salle?"

She smiled at him. "Yes, Papa. But I'm always happy to hear it again."

"I don't think it's ever run so smoothly."

It was nice of him to say so, but she doubted that was true. Problems arose constantly. Although maybe no one else noticed since she and Signora Elena took care of them.

Sebastian glanced back. An errant lock of auburn hair fell over one brow. "Don't tell her that, Papa," he said with a crooked grin. "The power has already gone to her head. Even Leo thinks so. He's heartbroken."

Heat crept into Francesca's cheeks. *Stupid cheeks.* Leo was one of Papa's fencing pupils who fawned over her. She didn't give a fig about any young man but Phillip, her Phillip, but she blushed at Sebi's baiting all the same. Sebi laughed.

Francesca tried to control her cheeks, which only made the blushing worse. Antonio joined in the laughter.

Francesca straightened her shoulders. "Remember who orders our provisions before making fun of me—if you ever want a steak again."

Sebi feigned being pained. "See what I mean, Papa."

"Enough," Papa said.

As Francesca came alongside him, he nodded sympathetically, leaned over, and patted her wrist. He and Signora Elena were the only ones who knew how much she still loved and missed Phillip, and that she'd never see him again. She sagged in the saddle, the loss of Phillip and Catalina carving a hole in her heart.

They rode on, the rhythmic clop of the horses' hooves the only sound. Slowly the mist thinned.

A wraithlike tombstone came into focus to their left.

The Church of the Madonna dell'Acqua's bell tower loomed out of the mist, its usually cheery red-gold color dark and ominous this morning.

"We're here," Papa announced.

Foreboding rushed back over Francesca. She shivered as she and her family dismounted. They let the horses loose to crop grass in the swirling mist among scattered tombstones.

As they headed behind the church, she took Papa's arm. It felt reassuringly solid, and her fingers tightened. She looked up at him. "Papa," she said, hearing the anxiety in her voice.

He patted her hand. "Not to worry, my Cesca. This will be quick. Then we can visit your mother."

She nodded and forced a smile. There was no point in worrying him. *He's right. He always is.*

Francesca's mother was buried in the cemetery where the horses wandered. Although Francesca had never known her mother, she usually felt close to her here, as if something of her spirit remained in the russet stones of the church, the swelling green hills, and the murmur of the Arno River nearby. But not today.

When they rounded the church, Signore Tarrentino, Papa's opponent, stood in the open amid thinning fog. He wore a powdered wig and a sneer curled his lips. He ran a hand down his embroidered blue velvet waistcoat.

Finery won't help you here, thought Francesca.

Rumor at the salle had it that he was the youngest son of some disgraced, minor baron. The Signore had grown up poor but had blackmailed his way to a villa and a seat in the senate. He was rich now and made sure everyone knew it. Francesca wasn't one to listen to rumors, but he certainly looked the part with his showy clothes and superior attitude. And yesterday he'd proven himself a thug who lacked honor.

Market day had started so pleasantly. Her family and Signora Bianchi, or Elena, had taken the carriage to Cascina. Elena had chatted merrily. The day before, Elena and Francesca had assisted as the groundskeeper's wife gave birth to a burbling boy, which always made Elena happy.

When they arrived at the market, Antonio and Sebi bounded out of the vehicle to visit friends, setting the carriage rocking. Elena hurried off to Santi Ippolito to talk to the priest about the baby's christening. That left Papa and Francesca to wander the market stalls together.

The air felt like spring. The colorful canvas awnings on the stalls swayed in the breeze. People in their Sunday best filled the square and talked over the clucking of chickens, bleating of sheep, and shouts of the fishmongers. The bright smell of ripe fruits and vegetables mixed with the darker smells of the animals.

Francesca had a long list of supplies needed for the school's pantry, so she and Papa moved from stall to stall and chatted with the vendors, sharing news and jokes, and haggling over prices.

She had never been more content than the last few months. Her afternoons were jam-packed with chores and lessons. There were so much to attend to as Mistress of the Salle that sometimes her head whirled. But after dinner she would have a wild gallop on Achilles across the hillsides to clear her mind before getting back to work. At night she would flop exhausted into bed. But the mornings, mornings were heaven.

She would rush down the stairs to join her brothers and the other students outside in the courtyard for fencing lessons from Papa. Joining the class hadn't been easy. Many of the young men resented having a girl among them. A few even left the school. Others refused to work with her, but some students didn't seem to mind, and several, like Leo, developed crushes on her after she beat them. Win or lose, training with Papa made her happy.

She was in a light-hearted mood as she and Papa headed to the cheesemaker's stall, munching crisp apples. They laughed, dodging a dog with a loaf of bread in its mouth chased by a bunch of rowdy children.

Papa had just hailed the cheesemaker when they heard cries and shouts behind them. They turned to look, but a crowd had formed so all Francesca saw was people's backs. A *thwack* and a shriek of pain rang out.

Papa's face clouded and he moved toward the crowd. Francesca followed, her stomach tightening. As more *thwacks* and yelps followed, the crowd murmured. Papa pushed through the people with Francesca behind him.

When they reached the center, she gasped. Tarrentino, red-faced, wielded a dark wood cane with a silver head. At his feet lay a chocolate-skinned boy of about twelve. For a moment Francesca thought the boy was dead, but his chest moved slightly. The boy's forearm bent at an unnatural angle, obviously broken. Raised welts on his face and neck darkened to blue-red.

Tarrentino raised the cane to swing again, but Papa caught it mid-air. Tarrentino tried to yank it away, but Papa held on.

"Let go!" shouted Tarrentino.

"I'll not let you beat this boy further," Papa growled.

Tarrentino sputtered and shook with rage. "That's my property. I'll punish it any way I like."

"This is not punishment," Papa replied. "This is murder." He turned to Francesca. "Get the boy out of here. Take him to the physician."

She nodded and hurried to the boy's side.

"Damn you! I'll have you up for theft!" blustered Tarrentino.

The boy's eyelids fluttered. He groaned as Francesca got an arm under his slight form and raised him to his feet. He collapsed, but a young man in the crowd grabbed the boy's legs and helped Francesca carry him out.

"You can collect him tomorrow at the doctor's office," Papa said. "After you've calmed down and he's been seen to."

As she worked her way through the crowd, Francesca heard Tarrentino shout, "This insult demands satisfaction!"

"So be it," Papa replied.

So here they were, on this cold, gloomy morning.

Francesca wondered what could have possessed Tarrentino to challenge a fencing maestro. Tarrentino was a politician, not a soldier, barely passable with a blade. He had no hope of winning. *But even beginners get lucky sometimes.*

Next to Tarrentino stood his two seconds, almost equally as foppish in satin finery. They too wore wigs and blades that, from their high sheen, looked more decorative than functional. The seconds rubbed their hands and stamped their feet to keep warm. With them stood Signore Russo, a white-haired, solemn man in a tan cloak who would officiate the duel.

The maestro squeezed Francesca's hand and disengaged it from his arm. She went to Antonio, who draped one side of his charcoal cloak over her shoulder, giving her a glimpse of the sword that hung at his hip. She huddled into his side for warmth.

Francesca wished she wore a sword. She craved a pommel to finger, a hilt to grasp, something to relieve her anxious tension, but Papa had forbidden it. Few people outside the school knew about Francesca's fencing, and Papa wanted to keep it that way as long as possible.

"Don't look so worried," Antonio said. "He'll be fine."

Antonio had Papa's grey eyes, black hair, and high cheekbones. He shared Papa's confidence as well.

"I know he will," she replied, trying to believe it. She rubbed her hands for warmth as Sebastian came along side them. Sebastian also wore a sword.

"I wish I had a sword," Francesca murmured.

"You know the law," Sebi said.

"I don't want to use it, I just want to have it," she snapped testily.

While duels were technically against the law, it was seldom enforced. Judges tended to be lenient with a man who killed or injured another in a duel. If Antonio or Sebi, as Papa's seconds, were called upon to step in and fight, they could count on the court's indulgence. Not Francesca. Any woman who killed a man received a death sentence, no matter the circumstances.

"And anyway," she teased Sebi, "I'm better with a sword than you are."

"You can't prove that," Sebi said, with a smirk.

"Only because you'll no longer fence me."

Antonio laughed. "Precisely." He gave her a gentle squeeze. "You know there's never been a woman second."

"I know, I know." Francesca had no desire to hurt anyone, despite how much Tarrentino deserved it. But she'd had years of practice alone in her room before Papa finally agreed to teach her, and she'd spent hundreds of hours training since then. It was strange to think she'd never use her skills.

After speaking with Signore Russo for a moment, Papa approached Tarrentino.

"Apologize," Tarrentino demanded, "so we may all go home."

"I will not apologize for preventing a murder."

Papa removed the black cloak he wore over his brown jacket and breeches. Sebastian took the cloak and Papa pulled on a pair of leather fencing gloves. "Let's get on with it."

As the sun finally broke through the mist, Tarrentino slowly removed his velvet coat and handed it to one of his seconds. Tarrentino ran a thin hand over the ruffles at his throat and glanced around nervously, as if expecting something.

Signore Russo took his position between them. "Come, gentlemen, take your places."

"The weapons must be inspected," Tarrentino said.

"There's no need," Papa replied. As the challenged party the choice of weapons was his. Tarrentino had no right to object.

"But I insist."

Annoyance showed on Papa's face as he handed his rapier to Signore Russo. The Signore took both weapons and gave them a cursory examination comparing their lengths and flexing the steel in his hands. He nodded and handed them back.

Papa fell gracefully into *en garde* position, knees bent, weight centered, blade pointed at Tarrentino's heart.

"The rules must be stated." Tarrentino plucked at his collar.

Francesca's fingers tightened on Antonio's arm. If there was no way to avoid this duel, she wished it would be over quickly. The man seemed to be stalling, but why? Was he too cowardly to draw his blade?

"We all know the rules," Papa said. He looked around the gathering then focused on Tarrentino. "We fight until first blood is drawn. Now get on with it, unless you've come to your senses."

Tarrentino reluctantly took his stance. The men saluted each other by raising the tips of their blades vertically toward the lightening sky, pointing them at each other, then slashing them toward the ground. Tarrentino's eyes flicked right and left as Signore Russo called, "Begin!"

ABOUT THE AUTHOR

Catherine Thrush is a creative powerhouse. She has worked as a glass artist, an illustrator, a web designer, a screenwriter, and a novelist. She wrote her first book, Quest of the Faes at the age of eighteen. It was published while she was in college working toward her studio art degree. Her screenplay and historical fiction manuscript, Lady Blade, have won several contests and led to her continuing work writing the Lady Blade series of novels.

Catherine took up fencing with Salle DeCesare in her twenties and has been studying it ever since.

She and her husband Thomas Thrush founded the company Urban Realms to sell books and products they've created related to RPG gaming—one of their favorite hobbies.

Originally from Wisconsin, Catherine and her husband Tom lived in California for many years, and now call Portugal home.

BOOKS IN THE LADY BLADE SERIES

Prologue – *Before the Blade*
Book One – *The Maestro's Daughter*
Book Two – *Lady Blade*
Additional RPG Game – *Lady Blade's Jaguar Jungle*

OTHER BOOKS BY CATHERINE THRUSH

A New Look at Old Words
Quest of the Faes

www.ingramcontent.com/pod-product-compliance
Lightning Source LLC
Chambersburg PA
CBHW031310280626
47169CB00017B/1184